War of Mages

The Tales of Drendil

Fallen Stars

The Collapse of Madira

Dark Magic

Raven's Requiem

The Manticore

The Murder

The Basilisk

The Minotaur

The Drendil Saga

War of Mages

Land of Madness

Siege of Shemont (Coming Soon)

Downfall

Road to Ruin

Scapegoat (Coming Soon)

War of Mages

B.T. Litell

Cover art by Cherie Fox at https://www.cheriefox.com/
Edited by Megan Hundley

First Published in 2024 by Ravensteel Publishing, LLC

Visit https://www.btlitellauthor.com for more information about the author and his projects.

ISBN: 978-1-7379624-2-7

Write to:
Ravensteel Publishing, LLC
PO Box 274
Canal Winchester, OH 43110

For anyone who had to choose the

greater good.

Trigger Warning:

This story involves depictions of war, fighting, death, and existential dread that may be too much for some. My intention is not to glorify or celebrate these but to show the humanity of those caught in the whirlwind others create.

Shimmering Ocean
Gilded Ocean
Anselin
Nahum
Vilyar
Sorcerer's College
Madira
Iron Holm
Erith
Amgan Fields
Shemont
Goblin Coast
Griffin's Perch

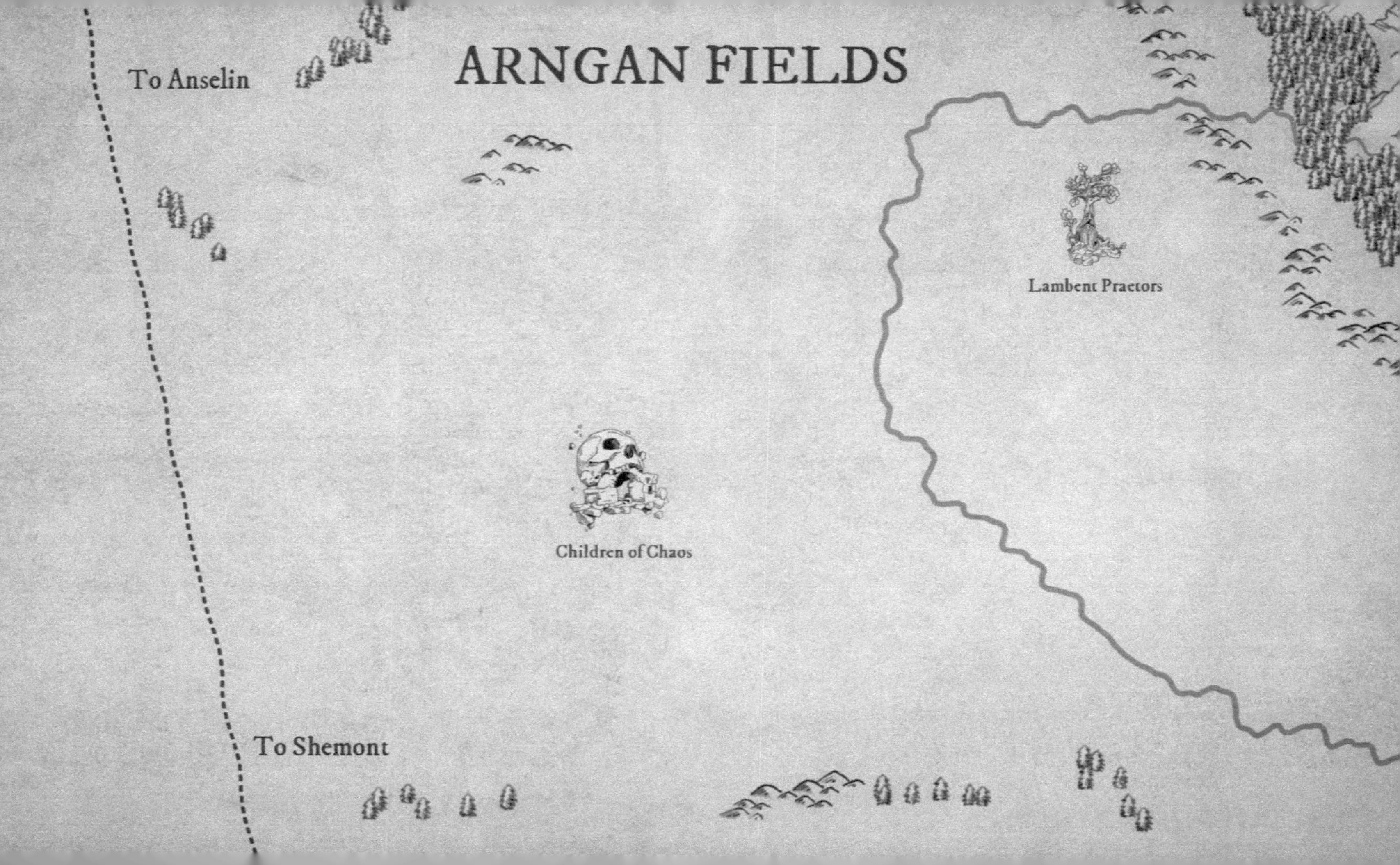

ARNGAN FIELDS
To Anselin
Lambent Praetors
Children of Chaos
To Shemont

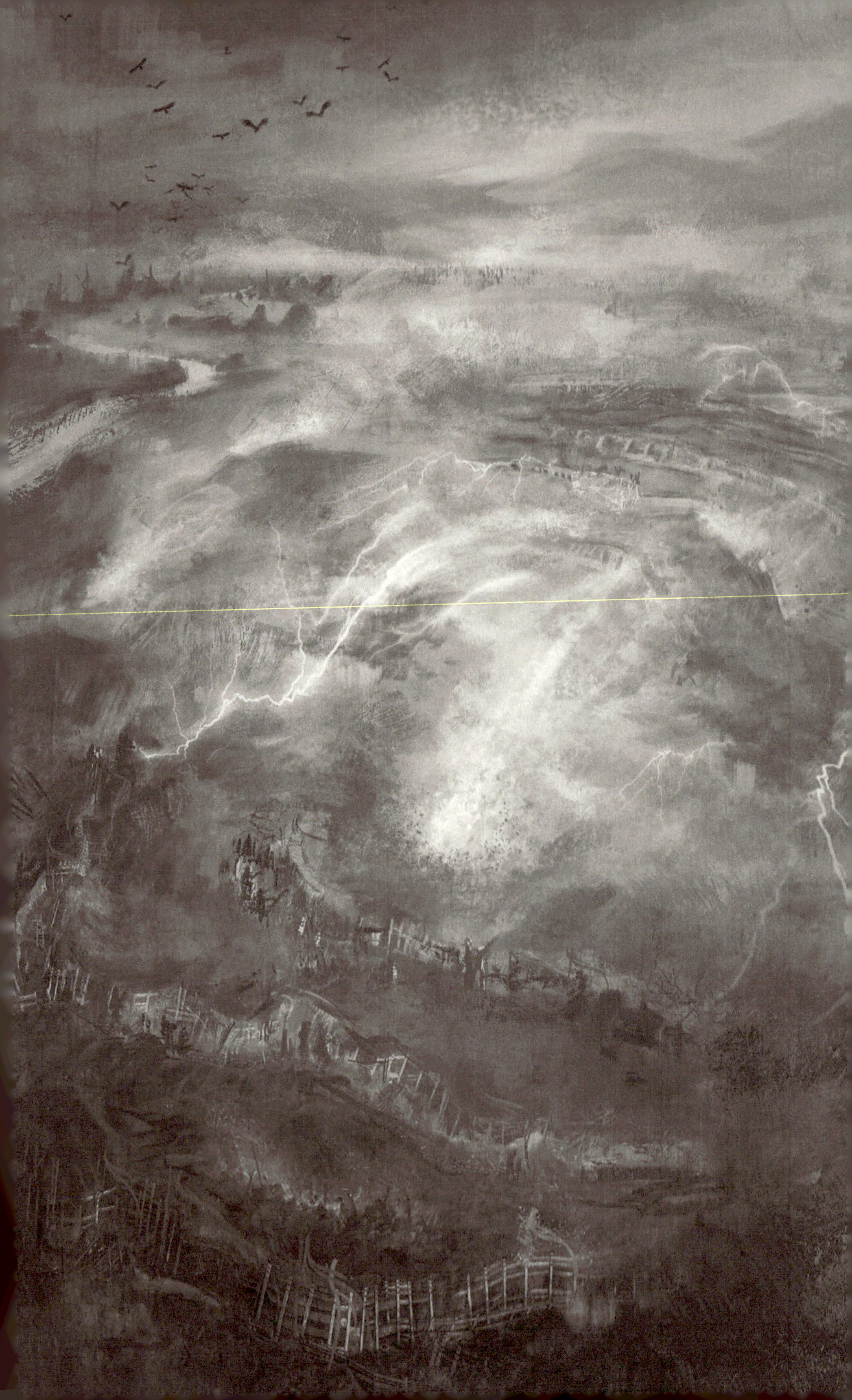

Table of Contents

Prologue

eldanna's stomach fluttered waiting for the assembly that Headmaster Gilros requested for, not only the Sorcerer's College, but all Mages across Drendil. Seldanna had never heard of such an assembly being called since the founding of the College. Not even Master Fylson demanded such a gathering, and legend told of his peculiarity. Between the sheer size of the crowd and her curiosity about the nature of the assembly, Seldanna didn't know what upset her more. Even a decade after the end of the Mages' War, she still fought against nightmares and paranoia from her time on the battlefield. The two years she spent as a village healer after the war wasn't distancing enough for her to forget the horrors she faced.

She took a deep, calming breath and counted to five before closing her eyes and exhaling slowly. She cleared the overwhelming thoughts from her mind and focused on her immediate surroundings. She paid particular attention to what she heard, smelled, and felt before looking at those around her for anyone she recognized. Despite her reintegration at the College a few years before, she still felt like such an outsider among the general population of Mages. Moments like this made her thankful for the friends she found in Troy, Virion, and Serena. All three helped soothe nerves and relieve stress in their own ways. She would need to spend some time with all three after this assembly. She closed her eyes and inhaled again, then as she exhaled, a gentle hand planted itself on her shoulder. She knew without looking that Virion had found her. Knowing she wouldn't have to suffer through this alone made her instantly feel better.

"I'm glad you found me," she said as she turned to hug her curly-haired friend.

"Here for you however you need it, Sel. Have you seen Serena?" Virion asked.

"I haven't. You didn't come together?"

"She said she would get here later. She's seemed distant lately, but I figure that's probably just the newer teacher end of year stress."

"Our students think their time during exams is difficult," Seldanna laughed.

"If they only knew."

Conversations quieted when a group of Mages dressed in their formal robes stepped onto a dais for all to see them. What little sunlight came through the overcast sky glinted on the polished metal armor accenting their clothing. Even this far from the front of the crowd, Seldanna knew these Mages were councilors. No one else in the College wore white robes with colored bands on the cuffs. After counting twice to be certain, she confirmed she and Virion only saw six Mages standing on the dais. The headmaster had not arrived yet but likely would within a few moments. The councilors seated themselves in the chairs placed on the dais, and Seldanna heard some of the Mages around her start chatting again. After a few seconds one of the councilors stood from their seat and started looking around, confusion in her movements as she strode to the end of the dais.

Seldanna's mind screamed that something was wrong, the words repeating, drowning out everything else. She pushed the thought away, dismissing it as another burst of residual paranoia from her short time fighting in the war. She wouldn't have thought just under a year on the battlefield could have such a strong impact on her. The thought returned as another councilor stood and joined the first, looking somewhere out of sight. Seldanna's heartbeat quickened, and her hands grew clammy. She clenched her robes in her lap to dry her palms but knew it would be for naught. Her right leg bounced involuntarily. She hoped Virion didn't notice any of this.

"What do you think they're looking for?" Virion asked, her question an attempt to soothe any fears that she may have noticed Seldanna's nervousness.

Before she could answer or go any further down the road toward panic, a portal opened on the dais opposite the standing councilors. Those standing turned toward the newly opened doorway in the air, while those still sitting turned their heads to look at the arrival. As the two standing councilors turned to face the portal, a bolt of lightning and a stream of fire jumped through the portal, catching two of the seated councilors and toppling them backwards off the platform. Seldanna's entire body tensed an instant before more destructive Magic poured through the portal. Now, several Mages in the crowd and the other councilors started moving into action. A flash of what looked like lightning but in color was darker than even a midnight sky shot forth and caught the standing female councilor squarely in her chest before jumping to her counterpart standing beside her.

Everything around Seldanna spun. She couldn't believe her eyes. This was obviously a dream. A nightmare. No one would randomly attack the Sorcerer's College with every associated Mage gathered at the request of the headmaster. Even considering such an event could only prove disastrous for the attackers. Yet, here she sat, hands clenched in her lap, leg bouncing, heart pounding in her ears, watching lives end and she could do nothing more than hyperventilate while her mouth filled with saliva and her stomach clenched. Sweat dripped into her eyes, but she hardly noticed the sting of the salt as reality tore itself in half before her.

Another stream of fire shot through the portal and a second later a giant man, his frame unmistakable from any distance, stepped through onto the dais. Troy. He took two steps onto the dais before casting another spell that engulfed the last councilor on the stage in flames.

Another Mage stepped through the portal. Flowing, auburn hair reached halfway down her back. Aska. Another stepped through, her silvery blonde hair cut just above her shoulders. Celeste. When the next Mage stepped through, her frame best described as willowy, Seldanna's heart sank. Serena. How was she standing with anyone responsible for such an attack. They must be holding her against her will. She's there to bait out a response. Seldanna timidly reached over and put her hand on Virion's in hopes of providing comfort but withdrew her hand quickly when she thought she grabbed ice. She looked at her friend and saw a blank stare that replaced the joy, wonder, and hope she saw only a moment before. Seldanna couldn't stop the tears from streaming down her face if she wanted. As much as they could deny why Serena was among the attackers, throwing a ball of fire at the last living member of the council, neither of them could ignore that she chose her place.

Seldanna watched others around her attempt to stand. Anyone who rose more than a hand from their seat was violently forced back down by an unseen force. Seldanna felt it against her shoulders without attempting to resist whatever Troy and the others would call this hostility. The force grew stronger, making Seldanna want to sink into the chair, collapsing into herself. She wondered if this sensation was only in her head, but she saw others around her squirm under this unseen weight.

Another Mage stepped through the portal. Seldanna knew Lillis but had never really interacted with her beyond a friendly greeting when they crossed paths. She held something in her left hand which trailed behind her through the portal. The other Mages parted to create a path for her and as she started walking, she wrenched the cord in her hand. She reached the middle of the dais as Headmaster Gilros, bound at the wrists by the leash Lillis held, stepped through the portal before it closed behind him. Seldanna had never seen him so disheveled before. Blood matted his hair, streaked down his face, and stained the tattered clothes he wore. Bruises covered his body, and he slouched and limped where normally he walked at his full height. Lillis impatiently snapped the leash in her hands, pulling Gilros forward harshly.

"What is the meaning of this display?" a voice called from the crowd.

"I bring a message to all Mages," Lillis called, her voice smooth and full of command. "This man wishes to limit your power, to make you fear *true* potential. We are here to set you free."

Before anyone could say another syllable, Lillis reached her right out toward Headmaster Gilros and gently caressed his cheek with the back of her fingers. Black spots spread from the tips of her fingers, devouring his flesh where he stood. He cried in agony until his throat was eaten by this curse. When he lost the last of his strength, he fell to the ground where he writhed for only a few seconds before going still. Within moments the rags he wore clung only to the bones this power rejected.

"Join us and unshackle yourself from this gross oppression. Their rules inhibit you. Cast aside their tyranny and see what Magic can truly accomplish," Lillis said.

She turned to where their portal had been and walked toward the same place on the dais. Without having cast another spell, Lillis, Troy, Serena, Aska, and Celeste all vanished leaving only destruction in their wake.

Chapter One

The decrepit stone structure, currently occupied by members of the Lambent Praetors' war council, muffled the rumbling thunder outside surprisingly well. After originally discovering Dark Mages about thirty years before, the decision was made to keep this building to house those requiring isolation from others. Seldanna despised that, decades before, someone deemed a dungeon necessary, let alone that it saw frequent enough use that no one leveled this building after that initial re-use of this ancient structure. Life would be simpler if Mages only needed to focus on learning, studying, and advancing Magic. Unfortunately, life never worked so accordingly, she reminded herself. Often the actions of a select few individuals ruin things for the larger population.

Besides the depressing mood clinging to the dungeon, the forced separation from her Magic left her feeling naked. She would almost prefer standing before the Lambent Praetors' war council with naught a thread covering her body. She knew the boundary spells that blocked Magic within the dungeon became necessary long ago, but she hated watching that light within her mind disappear like a candle burning one moment and snuffed out the next. The original safety net of spells only covered the cells themselves, but, after that first prisoner's thwarted escape, the College extended those spells to the rest of the building. Anyone stepping through the iron door upstairs lost their connection to Magic. Even the guards who once worked here said they felt something after entering the building, and they were Magic sensitive at best.

In the decades that passed since that first prisoner occupied one of the cells on the other side of the door to Seldanna's left, so much within the world changed. Unknown sects of Dark Mages performed rituals and experiments and, while the College knew of at least some of those groups, Seldanna found herself wondering just how much was still unknown about what the early Dark Mages did. At the very least, she knew they opened portals to other worlds, created one entirely new species, brought monsters into this world, and started wars. Allfather above she hoped that was all they did in the shadows. Chaos swarmed around the Dark Mages like flies on cattle. Worse than that, sickness and death now spread through Drendil faster than ever before. It started with the Dark Mages but spread from their ranks, infecting the world around them. People lost their minds, often without warning, taken over by something unknown and unseen. No cure existed for Madness. The priests in Erith thought they could save the world, but Seldanna doubted those codgers' abilities when the entirety of the College couldn't unravel this mysterious ailment.

Seldanna shuddered, an icy chill washed over her like the surprise touch of a cold hand against bare skin. She felt the same sensation when a healer's spell touched her skin. The small hairs on the back of her neck stood and goosebumps rushed across her arms and legs. Scratching inside her ear, Seldanna looked around to see if either Virion or Radelia noticed her shiver, but both seemed too preoccupied to notice. Radelia paced across the width of the room, the thick soles of her boots thumping against the damp floor. She took five steps before stopping, turning around, and walking another five steps. Seldanna figured at this pace Radelia might wear a rut into the floor before Conall returned. Virion absentmindedly chewed at the skin around her thumbnail while staring at the flame that danced atop the candle in the center of the rickety table where she and Seldanna sat. With the candlelight dancing on her round face framed by her short, black ringlets of hair, Virion looked childlike. Her dark brown eyes looked at the candle in the center of the table, but she stared miles into the distance, seeing nothing around her.

Radelia reached the far wall, and her boots whispered on the floor as she spun on the ball of her feet. Seldanna opened her mouth, frustration from the incessant pacing finally getting to her, but before her voice formed any words, the door at the top of the stairs moaned on its rusty hinges. Radelia stopped mid-step, and she and Seldanna both looked toward the staircase. They heard the shuffle of feet and the door wailed again before the latch clicked. It only took a few moments before Conall appeared at the landing that separated the two flights of stairs before continuing down to the main dungeon floor. If she didn't know him better, she might have assumed he had a spring in his step, but after blinking and rubbing her eyes, she now thought she was simply tired. When did she sleep last?

Conall looked around briefly and when he spoke, his voice stayed cool and level. "Seldanna, come with me."

Saying nothing, she stood and walked with him to the small side room to her right on the other side of Radelia's pacing path. The iron-bound wooden door whispered as it swung on its hinges. It seemed odd that this door would be more maintained than the outside door, but Seldanna quickly released that thought. Conall held the door open and motioned Seldanna to enter before him. Only a table and a single chair filled the small room. Seldanna stepped to her right to allow enough room for Conall to enter and close the door behind him.

"What's the plan, Conall?"

"I shouldn't have to spell it out, Seldanna. We captured the enemy leaders and will do what we must to end the war. Tonight."

A knot formed in Seldanna's stomach dreading what he might suggest. "You have so much confidence in your plan working, whatever it may be."

"Indeed," Conall nodded. He reached into his robes and removed a large, sheathed knife. "Dead Dark Mages can neither fight nor lead others to."

"You can't be serious. *This* is your plan?"

"This is the only way that will stop the fighting. We must act while we can."

"I don't even know how to respond to this, Conall."

"Well, that will certainly make this process easier. We don't need responses or debates. We don't need rhetoric. We need only to act."

Seldanna took a step toward the door and grabbed the handle. Conall grabbed her wrist before she could open the door. She brought her eyes from his white-knuckled grip on her arm to his face, staying mindful of the knife's location the entire time. Her hand ached under his intense grip, and while she felt his fingernails digging into her skin, his eyes showed no hint of emotion. Droplets of sweat formed on her brow, but she kept her eyes locked on his even as the sweat moved down her forehead and threatened to get into her eyes.

"This is barbaric and wrong, Conall," Seldanna said, her voice hoarse.

His already intense grip tightened on her wrist. "There is no right way to go about this."

"Let *go* of me. Now."

His grip loosened, but he didn't remove his hand. "You know this has to happen."

Seldanna pushed her shoulder into the thick wooden door, and as it started to open, Conall's hand released from her wrist. She stepped out of the small room with the simple table and chair as hurriedly as she could without looking panicked. Radelia now stood to Seldanna's left, at the other end of her pacing path. Her eyebrows scrunched, but she said nothing. Virion, still staring at the candle's fire as she continued chewing on her thumbnail, noticed nothing about the situation. Seldanna loved Virion and her almost innocence but wished that sometimes she could stay focused enough to be part of what's going on around her.

"You know this is wrong, Conall," Seldanna said standing at the bottom of the stairs.

"This was your idea. Finish what you started, Seldanna."

"What's happening?" Radelia asked, her face a mix of emotions.

"They are Dark Mages, but they still have rights. Your plan only circumvents that," Seldanna said, not wanting to even voice what Conall proposed.

"They lost those rights the moment they brought monsters and Madness into our world.. They started two wars. They mutilated innocents in the name of *creating* a new species, which they promptly discarded as waste. They betrayed not only us but our way of life. My solution is the only way we can stop them," Conall said, still holding the sheathed knife in his left hand.

Radelia looked from Conall to the knife to Seldanna. "Allfather's ear hairs will someone tell me what's happening?"

Fury hotter than a blacksmith's forge surged within Seldanna at the confirmation of what he planned. "There are always other options, Conall. You are the Archmage, not an executioner. Remove your blinders and look at this from another perspective."

"Again, Seldanna, this was *your* idea. I will end the war tonight however I can."

"There are reasons for our laws and courts, *Archmage*! You cannot sway me from this."

"Fine. If you want to stand by and watch others get their hands dirty, be my guest," Conall scoffed. "Radelia, your sister died in the trenches last year, correct?"

"Stabbing me with that knife would have hurt less, Conall. What a shit way to bring up that subject," the fiery-haired Mage spat.

"Have you reached closure about her death?" Conall said, walking across the room toward the door to the cells. Radelia visibly stiffened but said nothing. Her silence served as her answer. "Someone in those cells caused your sister's death. Justice is within your grasp. Seldanna grew cowardice with what she is calling a conscience. Will you side with her or find a way to ensure your sister's soul rests peacefully in the afterlife?"

Radelia's trembling hands clenched into fists and Seldanna heard knuckles popping. "You're such an ass, Conall, but if you put me in that room with those monsters, they will wish I was in the trenches instead of my sister."

"This isn't justice, Radelia, this is revenge," Seldanna fumed. "Hate blinds you both!"

"I'm not a coward though," Radelia said.

"How are we any better than them if we deny them mercy?"

Conall spat on the floor as he reached for the door handle. "Reverse this situation, and we would receive no mercy. They deserve none from us."

"I can't believe that you can stand there and—"

The door to the cell block slammed shut behind Conall and Radelia, stopping any further argument. Intense pressure built on Seldanna's molars, and she slammed her clenched fists against the tabletop. Her hands trembled and a furious growl emitted from deep within her being. The sound and impact from Seldanna striking the table startled Virion, who jumped, now broken from her trance the candle held on her. She looked around the room but saw no one else in the room with them.

"What's wrong, Seldanna?"

"You really did miss that whole interaction, didn't you?"

"Clearly. What happened?"

"It's Conall. He wants to—" Seldanna started to explain, but the door to the cells reopened.

Radelia stepped out of the cell block first followed by a slender woman wearing a burlap sack over her head. A coarse rope tightly bound her wrists together. Radelia held the other end of the rope like a leash, guiding the prisoner toward the other room where Conall revealed his knife. Even without seeing the prisoner's face, Seldanna knew this was Serena. She was Virion's wife before the Children of Chaos started the war. The Betrayal, the name they used for the catalyst event that started the war, caused Virion to withdraw into herself, becoming even less social than before. Even five years later, and all the fighting that passed, those closest to Virion thought she still had unresolved feelings about the situation. While her face showed no change of emotions, Seldanna saw the subtle way Virion's shoulders tensed at seeing her former wife in such a state. Her hands clenched in her lap, and she stared at the empty wall across the room instead of risking even glancing at Serena. Radelia opened the door on the other side of the room and pulled aggressively on the rope, forcing Serena to stumble into the room. The same moment that Radelia's coppery braid disappeared into the other room, Conall exited the cell block and forcefully closed the door behind him. He stood in front of the door glowering at Seldanna before walking to the other room and shutting the door behind him. A painful silence passed before Virion finally spoke. Her voice cracked and Seldanna thought she saw tears welling in her eyes but refusing to fall.

"Seldanna…"

"I'm so sorry, Virion. That was unfair of him to do that with you here."

"I appreciate your concern, Seldanna, but she stopped being my wife long before the war. Whatever event convinced her, not only to join, but to form this cult of theirs served as the catalyst. I have made what little peace I can with that."

"How can you sit there and act like you're fine with this, Virion?"

"Oh, I'm far from fine, Seldanna." Virion said, her lower lip trembling before she sighed then locked eyes with Seldanna. "Mages have been at war with our own kind for too long. Too many have died for no real gain. A brief time of peace happened between the wars, sure, but that only pushed us to where we are now."

"Conall is overstepping his—"

"Seldanna, this is truly a difficult situation to face. You have a strong grasp of this minor piece of the bigger picture, but if we are to bring peace to this world, we can't focus only on what happens here tonight. Everyone alive right now has lost so much because of this war. Can we truly rely on the politicians to find a solution?"

"It's wrong, though," Seldanna said, standing from her chair.

"On paper, perhaps, but what the Children have done is also wrong."

"If we allow this to happen, we are no different than the Children, Virion."

"Would you prefer to be better than them or alive?"

"How can we truly live if we cast aside our morality?"

"If we don't stop this war, the Madness they brought will devour the world. I can't sit here and say that five Dark Mages dying in a dungeon outside the sight of the legal system is worse than everything they've done. Can you? This pales in comparison to the list of atrocities they caused. Even ignoring their attempt to cull the species they created, this is a far lesser evil."

"Lesser, but evil all the same," Seldanna said.

Virion fell silent and stared at the candle before she eventually looked back up at Seldanna. "I may have a solution for you. It won't change what's happening in that room, but it should help you cope at least."

A shrill, agonized scream broke through the iron-bound wooden door to the other room. The scream seemed to echo through the dungeon. The echo seemed to grow louder as Virion, the table, the candle dripping wax, and everything…jolted. Shifted. Faded.

Chapter Two

…In the present…

Fat raindrops splattered against the beveled glass window above Seldanna's bed. The thick curtains covering the window normally muffled the sound of wind and rain, so any sound coming through meant this storm was stronger than most others. Seldanna stirred and groaned, not ready to be awake but knowing she wouldn't be able to get back to sleep with the unusual noise. She could hear only the rain against her window and her heart pounding inside her ears, the sound reminding her of a time when she worried about others breaking into her room. Her breathing grew rapid and shallow. Her hands clenched the scratchy, wool blanket that covered her, tightening to the point they hurt. The room spun around her, threatening to throw her from her bed. Before the swelling panic fully sank its talons into her, Seldanna took a deep, calming breath as she counted to ten then held it for five seconds. She focused on calming the whirlwind of thoughts and listened to and identified each unique sound in her room. Rain and wind against her window. The ticking mechanism in the small, brass clock sitting on a table across the room beside her wardrobe. The faintest whisper of the curtains above her bed as the draft subtly rustled them. When she was unable to identify any other sounds, she focused on what she could feel as she slowly released another breath. *Where did this dream come from?* It felt vaguely like a memory, but she thought she would remember something so awful. The shock of that moment, that time in a dungeon with the Children of Chaos felt too specific and horrifying to be anything but a memory. She pushed away the fixating thoughts and resumed her calming exercises. A minute passed before the timpani of her heart returned to normal.

Despite the chill in the room, sweat collected on her palms. She wiped them on her blanket, but they remained just as damp. After slowly exhaling again, she whipped her blanket off and sat up. She blinked repeatedly, but the darkness in her room refused to yield. After shifting her feet onto the floor, Seldanna cast a spell that made a fist-sized, translucent blue-white orb which floated in the middle of the room. It cast enough light that she could see, while staying dim enough she did not need to shield her eyes while they adjusted. Over a decade ago, when she first moved into this room, she set a spell on the floor that maintained a consistent temperature no matter the time of year.

Nothing felt worse than a cold floor against bare feet, and this room had only a small area rug between the bed and the door. The wood floor retained no heat, especially in the winter. She placed other spells throughout the room that served their own separate purposes. Only one served as her safety net, and she thanked the Allfather every day that one went unused.

Seldanna sat on the edge of her bed, hands folded in her lap and feet resting on the bare floor. Her eyes focused on an imaginary point on the wall beside her bed, but she didn't see the painted plaster wall that showed the faintest signs of cracks forming on the surface. Misty glimpses of the past filled her vision, and the events they showed her felt both unknown but with unexpected familiarity. She wondered if this is how it felt to see an estranged family member after years of separation and the cruel touch of time mutated both memory and features.

Still, these felt like...her own memories. They couldn't be anything else. She knew the faces of those in that dungeon with her in the dream that woke her. She fought alongside them during the war. Even today, three decades later, they were her colleagues. She saw Virion with her deceptive appearance of perpetual youth accompanied by her nervousness. She always admired that boyishness in Conall's face, despite the anger that flooded his eyes in that horrid nightmare. For as long as Seldanna knew her, Radelia stood rigidly and carried herself with such a commanding presence, both physically and by her strong sense of morality. Despite being shorter than average, everyone knew when she walked in the room. Even with all of this, knowing the people who surrounded her in this memory, she couldn't recall when those events happened. In that way, her dream felt so oddly foreign to her. It seemed impossible that she could forget something so traumatic. The thought flitted briefly through her mind before fading into the ether. As that thought faded, its presence clinging no more successfully than mist in the morning sun's warmth, another appeared that stung her more.

No one could consider her a young woman anymore. She couldn't possibly expect to remember everything in her life with the same clarity as decades before. As if to catch her bullying mind in a lie, she glanced at the backs of her hands as they sat folded in her lap. She saw thin, wrinkled skin that seemed to cling to her bones. Pain welled up but she fought against the vain desire to mourn her youth. In her prime, words like "delicate" or "graceful" often described her. Now, the thought that anyone, let alone herself, could use "frail" for her description hurt more than she expected. Everyone aged; this was a natural part of living, she reminded herself, hoping this would calm the nagging in her mind. While Elves lived slightly longer than humans, they still aged. Even Mages, who seemed to age slower, still faced time's cruel touch eventually. As an Elven Mage, she could hope all she wanted for youthful beauty, but that could never bring it back. She wanted to push reality's grotesque bulk out of her way, to force it to take a seat while she frolicked carelessly.

Taking a deep breath, Seldanna stood and reached her arms toward the ceiling then bent at the waist to touch her toes. She relaxed and felt the clenched muscles loosen in her shoulders and back. She stretched like this every day, but today she needed it more than others. Her back popped in a few places, but she continued with her stretches the same as every morning. She wouldn't let these resurfaced memories upset her routine. After stretching for five minutes, she sat on the stool at the simple wooden table she used as a vanity and brushed her once-beautiful hair that long ago was a lovely mix of blonde and brown. The brown had long since turned to steely grey while the blonde lightened to sparkling silver that shimmered in any light. Like every other morning, she tied her hair up into a bun which sat firmly at the back of her head. She didn't see the point in spending more time than necessary on her hair when she wasn't seeking suitors. Finished with her hair, she walked to her wardrobe. Mages loved their robes for reasons she didn't fully understand, but she enjoyed the comfort they provided. Her robes were stark white with a wide stripe on each cuff made of six colors. Each color symbolized the different disciplines taught in the College. Besides students, every Mage at the College wore robes with colors matching their schools, but those on the council wore white robes with every color on their sleeves.

When a student graduated and earned the title of Mage, they chose their discipline. Not every Mage stayed here at the College, but they all worked together regardless of where in the world they lived. Some went to various cities throughout the kingdom where they served as advisors to rulers. The most skilled among them served the kings directly. Other Mages served as Battlemages with the army. Others became healers, either through spells or by selling herbs and potions to the sick. Some, like Seldanna, taught here at the College, preparing the next generation of Mages for their time in the bigger world.

Once dressed, Seldanna checked herself in the mirror hanging on the inside of her wardrobe door. She had one last task to see to before she could leave her room. She touched the Magic within her, the bright spot she envisioned in her mind, and severed the thread connecting her safety net spell and her door which would alert her to anyone who tried to enter while she slept. With that task finished, she opened the door, stepped into the hallway, and closed it behind her. Being an hour before she normally woke up, the halls of the College were deathly quiet. She stood listening outside of her room for a moment, checking for anything she might hear around her. Complete silence greeted her pointed ears until she stepped away from her room and could hear the whispering of her slippers on the bare floor. She found no reason to complain about the silence as it gave her a chance to think about her new memories in peace. The only sound she heard for her entire walk to the dining hall was her own footsteps muffled by the regularly spaced floor runners. Even with her councilor status, she knew Helena would throw a fit if Seldanna asked for food this early, but she could get a cup of tea without ruffling feathers. Tea might help. She had yet to find a situation where sitting down with a cup of tea and thinking wasn't a solution or a way to find one at least.

Entering the dining hall, Seldanna found Helena and requested a cup of tea. The broad-shouldered woman disappeared out of sight, moving with a grace that always surprised Seldanna. Helena returned seconds later with the requested tea. Seldanna's only preference for tea was the temperature. Flavor hardly mattered by comparison. The large cup rattled slightly on its saucer as she walked to her regular table at the back of the hall. This table allowed her to see everything in the room. While a single, large room formed the entire dining hall, stairs and a short wall divided the room into three progressively smaller levels. The main floor, the largest area in the hall, seated the student population who came in to eat as they wished during the service hours. Between the large student population and varied class schedules, this prevented overwhelming the kitchen staff during mealtimes. Teaching staff and other Mages occupied the middle section one level up where they could oversee the main hall. Up one more level, Councilors occupied the smallest portion of the room and could see over the entire hall. Despite the physical seating divisions, everyone ate the same food. Councilors, staff, and students prepared their food in the final room. The food service area and the scullery where everyone returned their dirty dishes served as the only real interaction between students and kitchen staff.

Once at her table on the top level, Seldanna watched members of the kitchen staff scamper all around as they prepared the dining hall for the coming breakfast service, driven by the sharp whip of Helena's tongue. Helena disappeared into an area of the kitchen out of sight, but a whisper of her voice still reached Seldanna's ears. No one who spent more than a day at the College could be surprised at the fact that Helena was a loud, austere woman who ran her domain as rigidly as a ship captain sailing on the distant seas' rough waves. Unlike those captains, Helena never raised a hand toward another person, especially not anyone who worked in the kitchen. Seldanna rarely experienced a negative social encounter with the half-Elf, but she also knew that Helena's tongue was the sharpest part of her.

Periodically sipping her tea, Seldanna considered her fresh memories. Conall. Radelia. Virion. Serena. She knew each person and their faces. She remembered the *smell* of the dank room with the shallow puddles that glistened in the various low spots in the uneven floor. She felt the cracked, peeling veneer on the surface of that wonky table. She remembered how it wobbled at anything firmer than a light touch. How could these memories feel so new when she knew the people in them so intimately? This mystery more than anything else plagued her mind. How could she forget such a miserable location for so long, only to suddenly remember it? None of this made sense. She took another sip of tea and gazed into the distance as more memories from the dungeon flashed through her mind. Virion sat to Seldanna's left with her hands folded in her lap and her right leg bounced endlessly. A single, unacknowledged tear crept down her cheek without any attempt to wipe it away. As it dripped off her cheek, her face hardened. She stood a moment later and stormed out of sight, running up the stairs toward fresh air.

Seldanna delved through these new memories until a small, brass bell chimed the start of breakfast. Seldanna continued to drink her still-steaming tea until she emptied the ceramic cup and only then considered getting up to fetch her food. She refused to rush toward food when she could get more tea at the same time. Her stomach needed further calming before eating anyway. She took another sip while her mind drifted into more of these memories. They floated near the surface of her mind, their view murky and distorted like she was trying to glimpse the bottom of a stagnant pond through the scum and algae.

Chapter Three

...Somewhere in the Past...

endrils of cream-colored lightning rippled through dense clouds far overhead. Moments later, thunder whispered at the world below from the heavens. Rain poured from the clouds at a steady pace. Puddles of water filled every footprint in the thick mud left by the boots of Battlemages. The unyielding rain drenched hair, clothes, the ground, and everything else within sight. This area of Drendil never saw so much constant precipitation and would likely remain a quagmire long after this war eventually finished. Seldanna hated that changing the ecosystem was among the list of consequences brought with this war. Casting spells often came with unseen repercussions that usually only affected the caster and that was typically only after prolonged use. With so many Mages constantly casting spells in such a geographically small area, it made sense that phenomena such as shifted weather patterns happened.

Seldanna took a step and, as her foot sank through inches of soaked topsoil, she felt the chill of the mud through her leather boot. She ignored the growing queasiness in her stomach at the sound her footsteps made and instead pushed forward. Removing her boot from the mud to take another step resulted in a heavy suction sound as the ground reluctantly released her foot. She imagined the trenches could only be worse if the mud in the camp was this bad. As that thought drifted into the ether, the sound of a distant explosion reminded her that being in the trenches was infinitely worse, even without the presence of any mud. Countless lives ended on the frontlines; the light of a person's soul snuffed out without any more consideration than if someone had extinguished a candle. Everyone in this camp lost friends in those trenches, and everyone in this camp felt the same nervousness as shifts of Battlemages cycled to and from the battlefield. Worry plagued the entire camp over who might not return from the battlefield. Seldanna wondered if anyone truly knew how closely death and the infinite darkness that followed it lurked across the battlefield. Those fighting knew the dangers they faced, yet they fought that much harder, their desperation to live pushing them to make increasingly aggressive choices. Carelessness bred under that desperation. Death accompanied the careless and thrived in that situation.

Lost in her thoughts, Seldanna snapped back to reality when someone shouted to her left. She looked toward the sound and saw four Mages carrying an occupied litter. A thick, wool blanket covered the occupant, and while that kept Seldanna from seeing who the Mages carried to the medical tent, she could see that blood soaked through the dark fabric. Her heart ached at the sight, even more so from the silence where normally screaming accompanied the wounded. Hope said the wounded Mage passed out from their injuries, but years of war left her jaded toward hoping too strongly. While the war council rarely fought on the frontlines, no one in the camp avoided exposure to the price the war demanded. Seldanna herself spent her own share of time in the trenches early in the war. As the Mages approached, Seldanna forcefully pulled her foot from the mud and removed herself from their path. As they passed her, the blanket shifted, and she glimpsed a bloody, ghostly pale face gazing up at the steel grey sky with eyes she knew saw nothing. Allfather above this needed to stop. How many more lives had to end?

"Seldanna, Conall needs us in the command tent," a voice both harsh and emotionless shouted from across a nearby intersection of makeshift paths cutting through the camp. Radelia's sudden call ripped Seldanna's attention away from the dead Mage she didn't recognize. More lightning danced across the sky.

"I was heading that way. Do you know what he needs?"

"Not a clue, but he sounded serious. We shouldn't keep him waiting."

Seldanna caught up to Radelia and together they moved toward the command tent. "Conall has yet to sound lighthearted since he became the Archmage."

"Fair point. I still want to avoid being the source for his irritation again."

Seldanna couldn't argue with that idea. As they walked toward the tent, Radelia lengthened her stride and pulled away from Seldanna. As her pace increased, her coppery braid bounced ever so slightly. No one had any difficulty finding Radelia in a crowd with the unique shade of her hair. The way she moved, even with the mud, looked unnatural to Seldanna. Her back was rigid like there was a steel rod in place of her spine. Her shoulders and hips showed no unnecessary movement as she walked. Her fists swung forward and back at her side as she stepped through the slough. Earlier in the war, wood planks covered the paths, but those long since disappeared, replaced by unrelenting mud. Mages moving toward her parted around Radelia as she walked in the middle of the walkway. If her vibrant hair didn't expose her location in a crowd, the gap around her would show Radelia's location well enough. One could hardly lose her in a crowd even on the battlefield, it turned out.

They reached the command tent after a short walk after cresting the small hill. This was the largest tent in the entire camp, not counting the dining tent. Like every other tent in the camp, the fabric was once-white with gold vertical stripes and accents. All around the bottom of the tent, rising a couple of feet from the ground was a solid layer of filth the canvas absorbed through the years of touching the ground. As the thick canvas flaps of the tent closed behind Seldanna, two others on the war council entered behind her. Seldanna sighed in relief knowing at least she wasn't the last to arrive. It was unnecessary to say Conall was a stickler for punctuality.

"It looks like we have everyone," Conall said, looking around the large oak table that he hunched over. "Let's get started then."

As became normal throughout the war, an impressively large map of Arngan Field lay unfurled on the table. Small, wooden flags marked various points around the map that were controlled by both sides of the war. Black flags marked positions held by the Children of Chaos, and the white ones showed the Lambent Praetors. The Praetors' flags used the same color scheme as the tents in this camp, while the enemy flags were only solid black. Conall, like his predecessors, not only refused to acknowledge that the Children of Chaos used their own sigil but also declined to use that name. Seldanna only ever heard him call them something like "traitors" or "the enemy." Not long after his ascension to the Archmage position, he forbade anyone on the war council to even speak of the Children in any manner that he felt justified their cult's existence. While he no longer verbally rebuked anyone who used that name, Seldanna knew hearing their name bothered him to no end.

"There better be a damn good reason for calling this off-schedule meeting, Conall," Neldor said, standing across the table from Seldanna. One of five Grand Warlocks on the war council, his demeanor was grimmer than Radelia's. His missing left eye and the accompanying scars that surrounded his empty eye socket made it difficult not to listen when he spoke. Seldanna assumed his appearance, intensified by his refusal to wear an eyepatch, was a major reason Conall never snapped at Neldor for his borderline insubordinate comments.

"We need to end the war," Conall said, still staring at the map and markers as if they would magically present the answer to him.

"The Children have a limited number of Mages. We outnumber them seven to one," Virion said without looking up from her stack of reports. "The numbers alone favor us."

"We have thrown thousands of Mages at them over the past five years, but we've effectively gained nothing. We may outnumber the Children, but they aren't bound to a moral code in battle like we are. Not only are their tactics overwhelmingly more aggressive, but they also use spells and powers we outlawed before the previous war started. I see no way for us to keep up with that no matter how many Battlemages we shove through the trenches," Olara said.

"Olara is right," Neldor said. "Numbers alone won't finish this war."

"What would you do then?" Conall asked without looking up from the map.

"We could loosen our moral standing in this. I'm not saying to embrace the Dark Magic they use, but if we allowed—"

Conall cut Neldor off before he could continue. "I won't allow that, and I won't tolerate anyone who does."

"Have we had any news of the treaty that the rumors mention?" Wollarr asked. He was the newest member of the war council and generally only listened during these meetings.

"Forget the damn politicians," Conall grumbled. "The first treaty they made did nothing to prevent us from ending up in this situation, a second won't do anything extra. The Mages in this tent and on our side of the battlefield are the only people we can safely rely on."

"Then what is your solution, Conall?" Neldor asked, folding his arms across his chest.

"I don't have one, that's why I called this meeting. We need to come up with a plan."

"Brilliant deduction, Archmage," Neldor said, not bothering to even hide his sarcasm.

Seldanna stared at the map as Neldor's comment brought the war council to bickering about that solution. The sounds of the war council's heated chatter within the tent faded from her ears as her vision centered on the Children's camp drawn on the map. Seeing the rough sketch on a separate piece of parchment sitting over the edge of the map she visualized their camp in her mind like she stood within it. Virion's scouts risked life and limb to get the details of the enemy camp right. Virion still mourned those scouts who never returned from their missions. While the Lambent Praetors built their camp to surround the command tent in a layer of defenses, the enemy seemed to use no semblance of order or follow any kind of pattern with their camp's layout. Children of Chaos accurately described them. The map showed their command tent at the back of their clustered tents completely open from the west. An idea opened within her mind like a flower blooming in the morning's growing sunlight.

"Why not send a team to their camp to capture their leadership?" The others chattering around the table drowned out the words as they left her lips. Her eyes widened when she realized she spoke without wanting herself to form words, let alone release them into the world. Still hunched over the table intensely staring at the map like it would slap him with a solution, Conall picked his head up as the sentence finished.

"Repeat that suggestion." he said, pushing away from the table to stand at his full height.

No one around the table at this moment would claim that Conall had an imposing presence. He was of aggressively moderate height and build. His shoulders were slightly broader than average and unlike Neldor, he had no gruff features that artificially added to his presence. In fact, his tousled, sandy hair and the boyish softness of his face would normally keep him on this side of intimidating. None of that mattered in this moment though, as Seldanna's brain slowly processed the words that fled her lips a moment before. As Conall stood at the table, the councilors stopped arguing. The command tent fell into a silence so glaring Seldanna thought she could grab onto it.

"What suggestion?" Virion asked. She stood two spots to Seldanna's right, halfway between her and Conall.

"Someone suggested that we capture the enemy leaders."

"Pah, such an idea is wrought with foolishness," Neldor spat.

"It's better than your idea," Radelia muttered.

"That was my suggestion, Conall," Seldanna blurted out. Again, words flung themselves from her lips involuntarily.

The look on Conall's face shifted from genuine confusion to utter shock so fast she could have slapped him with slower results. He blinked deliberately before returning his gaze to the maps on the table. He looked back at Seldanna, a wild curiosity she never saw before filling his eyes. His bright blue eyes squinted briefly as he seemed to stare into her soul. She wanted to hide from him, to crawl under the table and remove herself from the attention of the entire war council. Everyone except Virion stared directly at her, and Seldanna suspected Virion didn't only because she remained perpetually absorbed in her scouts' reports. Anything could happen around her and she would miss it.

"Why couldn't we do that?" Conall asked, his eyes once again darting back to the maps.

"Wait, you *like* my idea?"

"Of course. It's not the best idea we could run with, but it's better than nothing."

"Wait, you want to go through with this idea of *walking* into their camp and kidnapping the Children's leadership?" Neldor scoffed.

"Based on the intel we have from our scouts, it could work with the right planning," Virion said before the entire war council devolved again into further bickering.

Chapter Four

...In the present...

The round, ceramic plate felt warm to the touch. Seldanna didn't know when Helena decided to heat the dishes before giving them to her patrons, but it was one of many minor details that made Seldanna appreciate Helena running the kitchen. Helena was a stern woman, and sometimes the sounds of her shouting made others wonder about the quality of life for the rest of the kitchen staff. Those who worked for Helena never filed complaints, so Conall simply let her run the kitchen as she saw best. Seldanna never saw any signs that those in the kitchen or scullery were afraid to raise a complaint either. Their eyes held no dread toward their situation.

For simplicity, the College offered most meals in a buffet style with multiple options making up the different meals the kitchen served. For staff and councilors, there was also the choice to order specific food if desired, but that came with an extra cost that Seldanna rarely enjoyed paying. The available options gave enough potential for variety that she could be adventurous if she wanted. As was the case with many other aspects of her life, she clung desperately to patterns and routine. Deviations from her patterns, especially when unplanned or unanticipated, not only annoyed her, but also caused a level of anxiety she never desired for anyone else to experience. Her typical breakfast consisted of two eggs, two sausages, spiced potatoes, and a bowl of whatever seasonal fruit Helena provided. While Seldanna stuck to patterns but also knew unflinchingly demanding the same fruit throughout the year was unreasonable.

After plating her food, Seldanna prepared another cup of tea and returned to her table, her perch from where she could watch over the entire dining hall. Thinking of this spot as such did make her feel like a hawk sitting on a tree branch as it watched for any signs of movement, but she preferred to know what happened around her over being surprised by the unexpected. Most mornings, again rigidly sticking to her patterns, she ate alone. While she didn't mind socializing with others, she rarely found herself in the mood for such interactions in the mornings. She knew others would conjure thinly veiled excuses such as not being awake enough this early in the morning or needing to ingest a certain threshold of tea first, but Seldanna never hid behind those pretexts. Few situations necessitated that she converse with anyone while eating, and she would never complain if that remained the norm.

"Good morning, councilor," a cheerful voice said behind Seldanna as she approached the council's reserved area within the dining hall.

"Good morning, Elisen." Seldanna said, her voice flat but free of the mild, involuntary annoyance she felt inside. Elisen was at least decent company to share her morning with, even if she was a bit chatty.

"Did you sleep well?"

"I could say I did, but lying isn't a quality I admire in others nor one I tolerate in myself."

"Did the rain keep you up? I sleep better when it rains. My windows are drafty though, so my room gets colder than I'd prefer."

"Would you like to sit with me, Elisen?" Seldanna asked, standing on the steps separating the staff and councilor areas.

"Oh, I would be honored, councilor," Elisen said with a slight bounce in the two steps she took toward the stairs.

Seldanna set her plate and teacup on the table, then sat in her chair and motioned toward the seat across the table. She may have wanted solitude, but she also couldn't bring herself to be rude and snub the young teacher. Elisen attained the rank of Master the year prior and was still learning her way around a classroom and likewise the College.

"I assumed you would enjoy a cooler room since you adore blankets so much."

"Well, the blankets certainly do help. I don't like that the floors get so cold though. The cold stings my feet when I get out of bed."

"You could use a spell to warm your floor. That's what I do."

"Oh, is it like how Helena warms the plates, so our food doesn't get cold as fast? That's a great idea, councilor."

"I suppose the principle is the same."

Elisen, a forkful of food between her plate and her mouth, stopped and frowned slightly at Seldanna, her head tilted playfully to her left. "You seem distracted."

Normally, such a prying question would annoy Seldanna, but she assumed Elisen intended well with her curiosity. Nothing in her hazel eyes seemed deceitful or malicious. A warning chirped in the back of her mind that before the Betrayal, none of the Children of Chaos acted unusually either. Seldanna silenced the thought after weighing that possibility for the briefest moment. She thought about Elisen's question and thought of the best way to approach her answer. Of course, she felt distracted by these resurfacing memories. How could she have forgotten what these memories showed her? There was no reasonable explanation for how something like that could happen. Even trying to think of a way to answer Elisen's simple question left Seldanna feeling distracted. Before she could form words, the younger Elf spoke.

"I'm sorry if my question was too personal. You don't have to answer if you don't want, I know you value privacy. We can just eat our breakfasts instead if you would prefer." Elisen said, looking down at her plate while a tinge of crimson flooded into her high-set cheeks.

"You have no reason to apologize, Elisen. It's entirely possible I'm looking too far into this," Seldanna said, looking at the surface of her tea.

She considered the nightmare that woke her this morning. Elisen, while starting this conversation, had asked for none of the weight that Seldanna bore to be dumped on her shoulders this early in the day. She had no reason to distrust Elisen, but Seldanna knew her less than others here at the College. She found herself wishing that Virion had gotten breakfast with her instead. Still, Elisen had asked, and sometimes having a person willing to listen was better than waiting for the right person. Seldanna chewed on a chunk of potato while she considered what to say.

"Have you ever *lost* memories only for them to return later with no explanation?"

"Not personally, but I know it's not unheard of. Some healers use spells to help patients recover from deeply traumatic experiences. I don't know how those work though. Have you seen a healer for something like that?"

"I don't remember doing that. Perhaps I can find something in the library about this."

"What are these memories about, if I can ask?"

"The war."

Elisen dropped her gaze back to her plate and idly pushed a piece of sausage with her fork. Thirty years passed since the end of the war, but discussing the subject still made many uncomfortable, and rightfully so. Seldanna, as a veteran of both wars, understood the desire to not openly speak of them. Elisen, however, was born shortly before the war ended, so she only learned of it through history classes here at the College. Seldanna considered that Elisen's discomfort for the subject likely came from lacking first-hand knowledge.

"I'm sorry for prying, Seldanna."

"It's fine. We can change the subject if that would help you feel better."

Elisen nodded slightly before putting the small piece of sausage she played with in her mouth. "How many classes do you have today?"

"Two. The first is about the founding of the twin kingdoms."

"That sounds so dry. There are too many layers of politics surrounding that."

"A Mage needs to know more than casting spells, Elisen."

"But the students *enjoy* casting the spells."

"I don't strive for entertainment. Some do enjoy the history lessons."

"They're usually the stuffy students though. Sorry, I don't mean that as a jab toward you specifically, but more of a general statement."

"I fully understand it's dry, especially the parts surrounding politics and law."

"I'm so glad that you understand that I don't hate learning history, it's just not as interesting to me," Elisen said, spreading butter on a soft roll she ripped open. "What's your other lecture about? You've only mentioned one."

"The wars."

Elisen tensed again. "It seems like I'm just having one of those days."

"It's only a word, Elisen. It's also a subject students need to learn. Perhaps if they learn and understand the events that led to the wars, they can avoid repeating them later when they are in our place."

"Oh, I understand, Seldanna. I'm sure the students will enjoy that lecture more than the founding of the kingdoms."

"Meaning what, exactly?"

"Oh, you know, most of the time when students chat in the hallways, it's normally about war or battles," Elisen said before taking a bite of her bread.

"They gab about wars and fighting because their experience is limited to a classroom."

"We have avoided open conflict their whole lives. Students and instructors alike have not been in battle."

"This is why teaching about the wars is important."

"I'm not sure that I follow your meaning," Elisen said, grabbing another piece of sausage.

"You teach students to cast spells because that personally interests you. I choose to teach history because students leave here destined to become advisors across the twin kingdoms. *They* must be ready in the event we end up in a position where war is the only resolution to a situation. The spells you are teaching can save lives, but the lessons I teach might save our world from outright destruction."

Seldanna didn't wait to hear anything further from Elisen. Instead, she grabbed her dishes and walked toward the scullery at a pace that was neither hurried nor dawdling. She had no reason to look back to see if Elisen reacted or not. Sure, learning how to cast a stream of fire at an inert dummy was great fun, but Seldanna hoped that she could save the students from ever knowing how it felt to end a life with such spells. After placing her dishes on the small table outside the scullery, Seldanna left the dining area and walked through the writhing throng of students flooding the hallways as she made her way toward her classroom.

Chapter Five

Seldanna's robes whispered along the floor as she continued her steady pace through the hallways. More memories surrounded her, overlapping with what she saw. She walked through a white marble hall with a series of runners in varying colors and patterns, but her eyes saw muddy fields. She pictured blood-stained Battlemages who trudged through flooding trenches instead of students heading to their classes or to eat the morning meal. No matter which direction they ran, those Mages rushed headlong into danger. She heard the air overhead sizzle as meter-wide fireballs cast by the Children of Chaos soared through the air. Wherever these spheres landed, there was a splash of flames that spread until they eventually dissipated. A Battlemage rushing through the trench passed too close to where a fireball landed. Flames grabbed onto her sleeve and in a moment, she stopped running and smacked at her burning sleeve, desperate to extinguish the flames before they could spread further. Others behind her stopped, wanting to help her, but they only created a blockage in the trench. Stopping here for too long became dangerous, if only because it gave the Children a better chance of hitting a target, even if accidentally. More fire rained down, sent from the other end of the battlefield. A moment later, those in the trench were moving again.

Seldanna blinked and the vision of the trenches faded, replaced with the hallway full of students. Few of the students looked at her for long, but the looks she saw on their faces showed concern. Her cheeks felt moist, and when her fingers touched her face, the students' concern became clear. When did she start crying? She wiped her face dry with the striped cuffs of her sleeves and continued walking toward her classroom. While her lecture didn't start for another hour, she arrived early enough to prepare. Walking into her classroom, more memories from long ago flooded her vision as she descended the stairs on the outside of the classroom and made her way to the front of her classroom. She winced at the images she saw. Fighting. So much death filled the five years that followed the Betrayal, the catalyst event caused by the Dark Mages who sought knowledge and power beyond this world to bring about misery and destruction. They craved power and dominance but instead found corruption which blinded them. A maelstrom of rumors circulated about where and how the Children obtained their powers, but Seldanna dismissed most of what she heard.

Seldanna stood behind her podium at the front of the classroom, centered so every student could see her equally no matter where they sat in the room. Four rows of seven chairs faced her, each row on its own level that extended from wall to wall to make stairs. Her breath caught when she saw occupied seats before her when they should be empty. She shook her head, blinked repeatedly, and rubbed her eyes until stars swirled around her vision, which only made the faces of those sitting in the chairs change. Streaks of mud covered many, with others bearing bandages and splatters of blood they seemed unbothered by. Every face stared blankly at her, their eyes glazed over with a thick, milky whiteness. Each time she blinked, those faces changed, yet one fact stayed the same for every person she saw: they wore anguish and despair like a mask, the emotions raw and unshackled.

"Why are you here?" she asked with all the strength she could muster. Her voice still sounded weak and rasping despite her efforts.

They continued to stare at her, no change showing on their collective expressions. She heard no answer from them and wondered why she expected any. She blinked again and the seats in her classroom emptied except the middle five in the front row. Her knees buckled when she recognized their faces. If not for how tightly she held onto the side of her podium, this would have sent her to the floor. Despite the blood on their faces which obscured some of their features, she knew who they were. Serena and Celeste sat on the right with Troy and Aska on the left. In the middle seat, centered in the front row of her classroom sat Lillis. The Children of Chaos. These were the last faces she wanted to see. Before the war started, before the fighting and the killing, she counted these five among her friends. Many others throughout the College did, too. Together, corrupted by the promise of powers beyond what the College taught, understood, or allowed, these five started the events that set untold destruction in motion. Unblinking eyes that looked brighter compared to the cracked, dry blood covering their faces stared through Seldanna. The bottom of her vision blurred as she looked at them, and when she blinked, trails of warmth streamed down her face. The Children sought darkness and destruction, but she wondered how intensely they all wanted that. Had someone unwittingly convinced them this is what they wanted? She refused to think anyone was entirely beyond redemption.

Troy, large man that he was, cared deeply for those around him. She remembered going to him for comforting hugs after exceedingly stressful days. She thought she could still feel the warmth of his massive hands against her back and hear his heartbeat as her ear rested on his muscular chest. He intimidated so many who saw him, but Seldanna knew from the moment she saw his rare but boyish smile that no real threat lived in him. Looking at him now, sitting in a chair that barely contained him, every instance of his friendship seemed like the peeling façade of an abandoned building. The last time she saw him, his pale blue eyes burned with a foreign fire never seen there before. She remembered the twisted snarl on his face that made him seem no less than feral. There was no scrap of comfort left in him. No compassion. Everything about his past self wholly changed. Sometime after the Betrayal he braided his normally loose, tousled hair; the single plait hung down to his shoulders. She hardly recognized him.

"I want nothing to do with you," she whispered at the seats she knew no one occupied.

Each person who now sat before Seldanna seemed so drastically changed. Before the war, many described Aska as doe-like thanks to her large brown eyes that conveyed the sweet innocence of a deer found in the forests throughout Drendil. Seldanna remembered feeling envious of Aska's luscious, wavy, auburn hair that framed her round face perfectly. Everyone described her as reserved more than quiet, and when she spoke those around her listened intently. Her change seemed the most shocking. Much like Troy, none of her personality remained. A visible bloodlust unmatched by any of the others replaced her innocent aura. Even before the Betrayal, Seldanna knew Aska despised that others saw her that way. Perhaps joining the Children allowed her to break from that image. Seldanna wished she chose a different path.

Being a close friend to Virion, seeing Serena's image stung the most. Slender, barely beyond the verge of willowy, Serena flaunted an unbreakable grace in every situation. Seldanna spent many evenings dining with her and Virion. Those two were inseparable despite the drastic differences in their appearances and personalities. Outgoing and engaging, Serena commanded most social situations while Virion was perfectly content keeping company with animals instead of the group of people in any given room. When the Children broke away from the College, Virion overcorrected and secluded herself even further from others. Seldanna remained one of few with whom she openly spoke. It took a great deal of time for her to even acknowledge that her wife, not only voluntarily joined the ranks of the enemy, but also stood amongst their leaders. Seldanna found it unfair how beautiful Serena remained even through the war. How could a person who was so willing to hurt someone that close to them still look so stunning? Her face had the same appearance of ageless youth it had for years and there was no sign that color even started fading from her hair. There was speculation that Serena used a spell to mask her changed appearance, but like other rumors, Seldanna ignored them. Still, such a notion was not unheard of among some of the vainer Mages.

The last two, Celeste and Lillis, were somehow the least surprising of the group to have broken away from the College. As the younger sister, Celeste strove for any attention from deep inside the shadows of Lillis's personality. Seldanna often felt it was akin to watching a newborn foal hobbling behind her mother. Lillis was more certain of herself while Celeste stumbled about trying to match the mother's unchanged pace. Four years separated them, but they looked so similar that many mistook them for twins. They both shared the same straight, ashen blonde hair, pale skin, sapphire blue eyes, and the subtly pointed ears that announced their half-Elf heritage. Lillis kept her hair short, with the sides cut close and the top longer; Seldanna never remembered seeing Lillis's hair past her earlobes. Celeste, though, kept her hair cut at her shoulder and sometimes pulled back.

Tears flowed from Seldanna's eyes, and she continued blinking them away, but the vision of these five remained. Seldanna stared at the Children of Chaos sitting in the front row of seats in her classroom, their presence alone more than unnerving. She began to doubt if they were in these seats as a vision or if they regained some type of physical presence in this world. Standing at her lectern, her hands clenched on the sides of its slanted face, a lump formed in her throat. She tried to swallow it so the words she wanted to speak could leave her parched lips. *They're not here and would never hear her words,* she reminded herself. Logically, she knew the classroom before her remained empty, as it was earlier, but emotionally, that hardly mattered right now. This vision, their presence, the pit forming in her stomach as she gazed at their faces was more real than she thought possible. Seldanna wondered if this is how others felt when unexpectedly seeing former lovers.

Up to this point, too much of her life revolved around hearing and processing the hatred others expressed toward these five. That same hate took root and grew within her. Anger harbored deep within many in the College who rightfully blamed the Children for causing so much death and despair in this world. She knew they started the war, the fighting, and the pain, but an unfamiliar emotion welled within her, bubbling like a spring in the mountains. From a rarely visited, dark corner within herself, forgiveness rushed forth like a river, splashing and sloshing as it roared its desire to escape. Feeling that rush, she remembered a time in her childhood when she stood at the shoreline while waves crashed around her, the strength of the sea washing over her feet, reminding her how easily the sea could use the waves to claim her. There was nothing she could do to hold this torrent of emotions back. She closed her eyes and surrendered herself to the surge. An unseen weight deep within lifted from her, and when she opened her eyes again, she gasped when she saw the visages of the Children of Chaos now gathered directly around her lectern, the same blood-stained, blank stares piercing into her soul.

"I'm so sorry," she whispered. The words, brought forth by the storm raging inside her, surprised her. "You deserved better, and I was powerless to get that for you."

At the sound of her words, the apparitions closed their eyes and faded to mist before leaving her entirely. Once again, she found herself alone; her knees buckled a moment before she released her death grip on the sides of her lectern's slanted face. Crumpling to the ground, Seldanna knelt on her dais and leaned forward until her forehead and the tip of her nose rested on the floor, her hands beneath her, pressed into her chest. These visions, the memories of Mages who died in the war, and this rush of new, unfamiliar emotions left her confused and lost. She imagined this is what a stick felt like rushing down a river on its way to the sea. She had never experienced this before. What about today caused these memories to resurface and torment her?

"Councilor?" a soft, familiar voice called before the rushed pattering of feet approached. A slender, warm hand rested on Seldanna's back, its presence both comforting and unwelcome. "Are you injured? Do you need a healer?"

"I will be fine. Thank you for your concern, Clara," Seldanna muttered into the floor before she started her attempt to stand. She raised her head and felt the room teeter like a child's top as its speed decreased and the twirling grew unsteady. Her eyes snapped shut and soon the wobble calmed, then stopped.

"Don't rush yourself standing up, Councilor. I can help you to your feet."

"Yes, I think that is necessary," Seldanna said before her aided adventure to stand. "How long have you been here, Clara?"

"Only a few seconds. It sounded like you were talking to someone and when I didn't see anyone, I thought you were preparing for the lecture. I closed the door as you collapsed. I was scared you hit your head. How are you feeling?"

"I should be fine soon enough. Thank you for the concern."

The door to the classroom opened once more as other students arrived for today's history lecture. They entered the classroom slowly until they eventually filled all but five seats. Clara made her way toward her usual seat where moments before the image of Celeste sat. Before the door closed completely, Conall slipped through with the grace of a fox entering a chicken coop. He closed the door gently behind him and stood in the back of the classroom behind the farthest row of seats.

Over the years, Conall paid time's unrelenting tax just the same as everyone else. The soft boyishness no longer showed on his face. His once wavy, sand-colored hair had receded, creeping away like waves at the beach. He stood the same height as he had as the Archmage in the command tent all those years ago, but only because he maintained the same rigidity in his posture instead of wilting like a plant in a drought. His gentle, amber eyes no longer sparkled with unrivaled joy but now looked tired. She found herself wondering if he was here for her evaluation but dismissed the thought. Regardless of his reason for stopping in her classroom today, she would teach in her same style. Much like herself, her students all benefitted from structure and routine. Deviating for Conall's sake would only throw off their studies.

"Good morning class," Seldanna said, greeting her students as she did every morning.

"Good morning, Councilor," the students said in near unison.

"It appears that Headmaster Conall is gracing us with his presence today."

"Seldanna, you flatter me. Please, continue teaching as if I weren't here. I am here only to observe," he said after some of the students turned their heads toward him.

"Very well," Seldanna said. "Today we will be discussing the Second Mages' War, specifically the events that brought about its end. I see there is already a question."

Adrian, one of the boys in the class who was slated to graduate within the year, had his hand raised. "Councilor, we have all heard the textbook lectures about the ending of the second war. The Treaty of Anselin, signed by King Elred, officially condemned the Children of Chaos for their atrocities."

"What is your question, Adrian?" Seldanna asked.

"Why would the Children of Chaos suddenly comply to a second treaty when their predecessors, the Assembly of Mages, signed the first treaty but continued studying Dark Magic in secret? It doesn't make sense to resort to another political solution to stop conflict."

Seldanna locked eyes with Adrian, curious where this train of thought came from as he was normally more level-headed. "You raise an interesting point, Adrian. Yes, the Treaty of Anselin brought about an official end to the war and the fighting, but a series of events led to that treaty's creation."

Leena, one of the Elves sitting in the front row raised her hand. "Councilor, were you there for the end of the war?"

Seldanna wiped her palms on her robes before answering the question. "I was."

"Could we hear your perspective of what ended the war?" Adrian asked. "The textbooks are bland with their content, and the library doesn't have many memoirs written by those who fought in the wars."

Seldanna's eyes shot to Conall in the back of her classroom. He shrugged his shoulders, giving her the choice to skirt around the questions if she chose. She took a deep breath through her nose before returning her attention to the students.

"War is a complicated topic, Adrian," she started. "Even when you find yourself in a situation where taking a life protects others, it's not one to make lightly. Every choice we make comes with consequences, many of which remain unseen for some time after. While there are memoirs from those who fought in the wars, many of us wish to put that time in our lives behind us and simply live a normal life."

"Councilor, did you ever kill someone in the war?" Ailas asked. Like Adrian, he was preparing for his graduation.

"Ailas, that's such a rude question to ask," Clara said, opening the door to criticism between those in the class. The class became lively as students chose sides.

"That's enough!" Seldanna said, her voice louder than she normally wished it to be. The class quieted and the students settled back into their seats. "I wish not to glamourize war and death. To that effect, Ailas, I not only won't answer your insensitive question but will ask that you not ask that of anyone again. My job, as I teach these topics about the wars, is not to excite you and make you long for an outbreak of needless killing—"

Conall interjected despite his earlier declaration. "Well said, councilor."

Seldanna continued speaking like Conall hadn't interjected. "I also understand that reading books about the wars is rarely enough. I earned the title of Mage near the end of the first war and spent much of my free time before then studying and reading about what happened up to that point. To answer your earlier question, Adrian, there are many who share your sentiment that words alone won't protect us from evil and that we must take matters into our own hands and save our world. After all, no one else will save the world if we sit on our hands, right?"

"Precisely. Words and paper only go so far," Adrian said.

"Well, let's talk about what happens when we take matters into our own hands and how that looks for those around us," Seldanna said.

Chapter Six

...In the past...

Seldanna's idea for capturing the Children of Chaos, while simple enough in theory, required extremely precise planning for it to have any chance of working. This operation required perfect, voluntary cooperation between everyone on the war council, a difficult feat to accomplish when so many egos stood in the command tent at the same time. Under times of less stress such a task would be daunting. Now, with so much at stake, Seldanna's head spun merely at the thought. All this planning relied on the accuracy of the information that Virion's scouts provided. They worked tirelessly to supply the most accurate details to support the war council's ability to make tactical decisions and better command the battlefield. These reports were by no means perfect, and some even conflicted with others, but the scouts did the best they could. Virion received their reports, sifted through the findings, and fed the council whatever information they needed. She had never tried to sway decisions with her findings or put her own spin on situations. She merely came to the tent and supplied data when requested. She hardly seemed bothered by how the council used what she gave them. Ultimately, everyone in this tent wanted the same result: the end of the war.

"This entire plan hinges on us getting to the Children's camp without them noticing us," Neldor said. "Our only hope to accomplish that is by sending a team west of their camp and tracing back east through Arngan Field. Even then, they'll likely spot whomever we send and this whole thing will be for nothing."

"Typical Neldor, complaining about problems without providing solutions," Radelia said, rolling her eyes with a hand firmly gripping the end of her braid.

"We don't need to send a massive force to their camp," Seldanna reminded. "If we send a few strong Mages, we can surprise them easier than if we send many middling ones."

"The question still remains how do we get *any number* of Mages into their camp undetected?" Neldor countered. "We could send our entire camp, but if they see us approaching, our operation fails before it even starts."

"We could portal in directly behind their command tent. It's practically unguarded from behind," Virion said.

"You're assuming they won't sense the portal as it opens. They're still Mages, and we can all tell when a spell is cast nearby," Neldor groaned.

"Then we mask the portal," Seldanna said.

Conall's face scrunched at the suggestion, and he glanced between Seldanna and Neldor looking for clarity. "What's that now?"

"It works no differently than our safety net we set up in the trenches as a precaution against us losing too much ground to the Children. Our spells are anchored so no one has to hold them open, and their locations are masked, so unless you're specifically looking for those spells in those areas, you won't have any idea they're even there until it's too late. The hope is they wouldn't think to check for traps in the trenches and by the time someone thinks about that it's too late," Seldanna explained. "This should work just the same…in theory."

"Is it even possible to mask a spell without anchoring it?" Radelia asked.

"Testing that should be simple enough," Virion commented, still not looking up from her reports to see if anyone heard her or cared that she said something.

"Seldanna, I appreciate that you suggested this plan, but I see too many uncertainties for me to officially sanction an operation," Conall said. Outside the tent a bell faintly tinkled announcing a meal was ready, and Conall looked around the table in confusion. "How long have we been here?"

"At least three hours," Virion said, the faintest splenetic tone in her voice. Conall seemed either not to notice that or decided to leave it alone.

"Right. In that case, we should break for food. That should allow us to clear our heads and come back with renewed ideas. Meet back here in an hour. Radelia, Seldanna, see if you can figure out the spell masking. How we plan this will have to wait for what you discover."

"Understood," Radelia said, looking at Seldanna.

Conall, with Neldor trailing closely behind, led the exodus from the tent. Seldanna always wondered what Neldor constantly whispered in the Archmage's ear as they walked together. Many others on the war council gave Conall a respectful berth, but Neldor seemed to follow him like a shadow. Seldanna and Radelia stayed behind while the others left to discuss their plan for the testing. Virion remained at the table, leafing through another stack of papers, likely another batch of reports from the scouts.

"Food or spells first?" Seldanna asked.

"I know we should eat, but I'm not hungry. Casting spells should work up an appetite."

"Certainly. I would rather give extra time for testing than to rush through that because we took too much time eating."

"Let's get to it. Care to join us, Virion?" Radelia asked.

Virion finally took her attention from her reports and looked around the empty tent in confusion, still holding the stack of papers. "You want me to go with you?"

"You could use a break. I know those reports are important, but you haven't been outside since you got here this morning, and you've got ink on your face, dear," Seldanna said.

"Oh," Virion said, more than a hint of shame in her voice as she set the reports on the table. She looked at her hands, only then seeing the splotches of ink on her fingertips. "I hadn't noticed before. I wish the ink didn't smudge so easily."

"The testing should be simple enough," Seldanna said. "Actually, if you come with us, that should make this easier."

"I'm happy to help where and how I can," she said. Seldanna disliked that the others treated Virion like she was an inconvenience, if they even noticed her at all. Most seemed to think of her no differently than a potted plant.

"I have an idea for what we can do. Let's get to my tent. We can do the testing there," Radelia suggested. When the trio left the command tent, the chill and the fierce wind cut through their layered clothing within moments.

*   *   *

Radelia's tent, like so many in the camp, was arranged perfectly between spacious and cramped. Those on the war council didn't share their tents with others when arrangements allowed, so that offered some extra room. Virion sat at the foot of Radelia's neatly made cot, her hands folded in her lap. The toes of her boots only just touched the floor. Radelia stood beside Virion, her fingers busily tying the strip of folded cloth they would use as a blindfold around Virion's eyes. Beside the cot was a small table with a single drawer. A candle, the orange-yellow flame dancing on the cotton wick, was the only thing currently on the table. The soft, warm light from the flame cast shadows in the far corners of the canvas tent. Seldanna stood across the width of the tent from Virion beside Radelia's simple, three-drawer dresser. Another candle sat on the dresser, but it was unlit; they didn't need much light for their testing. Seldanna took another look at Radelia's furniture and wondered if "simple" was too generous of a word.

"You're sure this will work?" Virion asked when Radelia finished tying the blindfold.

"Not in the slightest, but like anything else, it's worth a try. Is that too tight?"

"It's fine for now."

"Good. Can you see anything?" Radelia asked.

"I think it's darker wearing this than if I just closed my eyes."

"Well," Radelia said before pausing for a second, "that's what we need. Seldanna, are you ready?"

"As much as I ever will be. I'll open three portals. For the first, don't mask the spell. We want to make sure she knows when it opened," Seldanna said.

"That's probably better than what I was planning."

"Radelia, for any reliable testing, you need a standard to compare your data against," Virion said, turning toward the back of the tent where no one was.

"Well, now we know you can't see anything," Radelia said.

"You thought I lied?"

Seldanna sighed but cleared her mind and imagined her childhood bedroom. Portals were fickle spells, and you needed a specific idea of your destination, or they either didn't work or ended in disaster. In this case, they weren't walking through the portal, so it didn't matter, but she practiced like it did. She visualized the textured plaster walls, a plush rug in the center of the creaky, wooden floor, the rocking chair in the corner where her mother would sit to read bedtime stories, and the bed against the wall opposite the door with the loud hinges. Her bedding, pink and grey gingham, covered a firm but lumpy mattress. Sitting atop her down-filled blanket was her single pillow and Piotr, a stuffed toy rabbit her grandfather gave her when she was a toddler. For many years they were inseparable. After her grandfather's passing, she clung more tightly to her rabbit like it could bring him back to her.

With this thought locked in her mind, Seldanna crafted the portal spell. This was a simple spell that only took a second to build. When she finished, a transparent doorway opened in the middle of Radelia's tent. The ethereal edges shimmered just like air above an open fire. She saw through to the room on the other side, though she wished she couldn't. The room beyond, while still her childhood room, now looked decrepit after years of the house being abandoned. Dirt and grime covered every surface she could see. Piotr no longer sat on the bed, the rug wasn't fluffy but was now matted down and tangled like mangey fur on a stray dog, and she could see cobwebs on every surface, dust collecting in the abandoned homes of spiders long since dead.

"Did you feel that Virion?" Radelia asked, looking at the blindfolded Mage.

"Yes, I can tell someone cast a spell. It's still going too, right here," Virion said, pointing directly at the portal despite still talking at Radelia's dresser. Seldanna closed it after making eye contact with Radelia. "Oh, it's gone now. Was that part of the test?"

"Indeed," Seldanna said.

"What happens now?" Virion asked.

"Well, now I'll open a portal, but Radelia will mask it and we'll see how that goes."

"Won't I sense Radelia's spell though?"

"I hadn't thought about that," Radelia said. "Let's see how this goes, but we may need to rethink our process."

"No, this will work. The portal gives off a stronger presence than the masking spell. If it works, she should only sense your casting. If it doesn't, she'll feel both," Seldanna said.

"That makes sense. Virion, are you ready?"

"Does that matter?"

"Well," Radelia said before trailing off.

Seldanna started another portal spell with the image of her bedroom locked firmly in her mind. As she started the spell, Radelia added her part that would cover both openings of the portal. It would be counterproductive if the spell only covered one end, and a mistake like that would only result in killing whoever first stepped through the portal to the Children's camp. That wasn't an outcome anyone wanted. Undoubtedly, that would also lead to immediate, unforeseen consequences, likely in the form of increased aggression from the Children.

"Are you casting yet?" Virion asked.

"Yes, Radelia just finished her masking spell."

"Shouldn't I have sensed something when that happened?"

"You didn't feel anything?" Radelia asked, unable to hide the disbelief.

"I felt nothing. Is the portal open?"

As Virion asked, the doorway appeared in the air the same as before. "Now it's open."

"You're sure?" Virion asked. "I can't tell. If this weren't a serious situation, I would think you were both playing tricks on me like I was a schoolgirl again. How can some children be so cruel?"

"Well, this should please Conall, at least," Radelia said.

"Let's try it again to make sure. No offense, Virion, but I want to know for certain that we aren't sending anyone to the Children's camp only to die."

"Oh, I take no offense, Seldanna. One way to have definite proof, though, is for someone else to wear the blindfold. That would at least remove any potential doubt that this works."

Seldanna looked at Radelia and shrugged. "She has a point, you know."

"Yeah, she does. Come here, Virion. Let's get that blindfold off. I'll put it on, and we can test it again," Radelia sighed.

Chapter Seven

Every piece of furniture throughout the mess hall had seen many better days. Cracks ran through what parts of the thin varnish remained on the warped, wooden planks, while bare spots showed where plates and arms had rested on the tops of these tables for an untold number of years prior to finding their way to this canvas-walled battlefield tent. While a lantern sat on each table inside the tent, few of them cast any significant light, and shadows clung to most of the tent. The table Seldanna chose to eat at today didn't have a lit lantern, and right now she preferred that. At least this way, Virion wouldn't spend the whole meal staring mindlessly at the flame as it danced on the wick inside the glass bubble. Her fascination with fire reminded Seldanna of when she was a student, and the boys around her age realized their interest in the girls and sought their attention. Seldanna hated to think of the pain Virion still felt all these years later after the Betrayal, but there was no doubt that she still dwelled on her former wife being a Child of Chaos. It seemed unlikely that anyone could forget about that, given how suddenly they formed.

Seldanna set the tray holding her simple plate of food on the table and pulled her chair out just enough that she could sit. The chair wobbled as if putting any amount of weight in the wrong place could cause it to fall apart with little warning. She sat into the chair as gingerly as possible and decided not to move it back under the table even though she wanted to sit more comfortably. Radelia sat to her left and Virion on her right. Four chairs sat around the table, just the same as every other table in the dining tent, and while anyone else was free to join them, the rest of the war council had already started eating elsewhere in the tent since they came here straight from the command tent without having to stop elsewhere and test spells. Seldanna looked toward the table where Neldor and Conall sat, talking but quiet enough not to be overheard even three tables away. She often wondered what Neldor whispered in Conall's ear but pushed the thought away and instead focused on those at the table with her.

An involuntary shiver raced up her spine when she caught a glimpse of Neldor's missing eye and the wicked scars surrounding the empty socket. She still couldn't believe he survived taking a lightning spell to the face and managed to only lose his eye. So many others who faced the same weren't even half as lucky. While everyone on the war council had battlefield experience from either earlier in this war, or from the first which ended not long before this one started, few would argue their experience to be close to as harrowing as Neldor's. No one else on the war council boasted such an obvious injury. Even though she only knew him without his eye, Seldanna still felt uncomfortable standing or sitting on his left side, as she was now, where she could see how far down the side of his head the scars stretched. The longest streak remained a solid streak until it passed his ear before it faded. Part of the discomfort she felt originated in how he seemed to lack a blind spot despite his missing eye. She never saw anyone sneak up on him even in the near decade she'd known him.

"Thank the Allfather I can't see him," Radelia said.

"What do you mean?" Seldanna asked, taking her eyes away from Neldor, and looking at the copper-haired Mage sitting beside her.

"Neldor's scars. I can't help but stare at them either. The more I look though the more unsettling it becomes."

"I wasn't staring at them," Seldanna said.

"You ignored my question."

"Alright, I was staring, but it wasn't on purpose. I…" Seldanna trailed off, dropping her eyes to her plate in shame.

"It's a mixture of curiosity and pity," Virion chimed in before her forkful of vegetables disappeared into her mouth.

"I'm not judging you, Seldanna," Radelia said. "He creeps me out."

Seldanna lifted her eyes and looked inquisitively at Radelia. "Why do you think that is?"

"He almost acts like his eye is still there. He should cover the hole in his face."

"Others have asked him to, but he ignores them or tells them off completely," Virion said, grabbing a chunk of boiled potato with her fork.

"I have a feeling he's going to shit on what we learned if only because it's *we* who are furthering this plan instead of him," Seldanna said. She used the side of her fork to cut a piece of the spongy chicken on her plate. "Gods in their realms the food is terrible!"

"I'm not sure what more you'd expect, honestly," Radelia said.

"It's the same cooking staff we had before the fighting started. Why was there such a drastic change between then and now?"

Radelia snorted briefly but said nothing. Virion's face scrunched before she answered. "That's a good question. The quality of our food is no different here than at the College, right?"

"It's this makeshift kitchen we have here. You have to remember that this *is* a battlefield after all," Radelia said right before the sound of artificial thunder boomed from outside the camp. Seldanna's cheeks warmed as she realized the sound was one of many that haunted the trenches, while she sat in relative safety, griping about the food before her.

"I suppose I should have fewer complaints," she said solemnly after a brief silence. "After all, the food is at least warm, and there are others with worse issues right now."

They ate the remainder of their meal in silence. Seldanna ate three more small bites of the dissatisfying chicken as penance for her comment before her jaw ached enough that she forced herself to stop.

She turned her plate to assess the rest of her food after she decided to ignore the rest of the meat. The potatoes looked to be the most edible food on her plate. She doubted anyone could incorrectly cook a root vegetable even if they tried. Her fork slid through a large chunk with relative ease, a needed relief. She ate, but after finishing that piece of potato, she lost her appetite. Thoughts raced through her head, and despite her best efforts she couldn't quiet them. Each focused on the upcoming operation, and none of these thoughts were positive. Conall liked her idea. That sentiment alone should be sufficient approval that she could cast aside her doubts and this fear that loomed over her like a cloud threatening to drown her in a torrential downpour. Sadly, her elation at winning his approval didn't last anywhere nearly long enough to keep out her thoughts of insufficiency. Not wanting to torture herself further, she set her silverware down on her plate and stared at the uneaten food.

Still wrestling with her thoughts, Seldanna moved back in her chair and turned away from the table, stood, grabbed her dishes, and headed toward the area of the tent that served as the scullery. Radelia and Virion followed, and soon all three were stepping through the thick canvas flaps of the tent back into the cold and blustery weather they dreaded. Rain continued falling despite the ground already being a sopping mess, their footsteps sloshing through thick mud that threatened to remove their tightly laced boots with every step. Radelia led the way with her perpetually abundant confidence, while Seldanna and Virion leaned against each other for support, struggling not to topple each other. More stretchers carrying wounded Battlemages passed down the makeshift road between the tents as the three Mages trudged back toward the command tent. Ahead of them, Radelia disappeared around a corner as the slick mud brought Virion down, landing in the mud face first with Seldanna swiftly dropping atop her. When Seldanna landed, she felt Virion's back pop and heard a faint noise that could only be her pained sigh as breath squeezed from her lungs. Seldanna awkwardly got to her knees and helped Virion roll to her side to free her face from the mud.

"I'm sorry, Seldanna. I don't know what happened," she gasped.

Seldanna helped Virion wipe some of the mud from her face. "You have no reason to apologize, especially since I landed on you. Are you hurt?"

"I'll be fine," she said, slowly sitting up. "I'm sore but not more than I can tolerate."

"Do you want to go to your tent to change?"

"I don't think anyone will notice. It's not like they ever do anyway."

Seldanna helped Virion get to her feet then hugged her. It was unfair that even before the war started others always looked through her. It hurt that Virion not only noticed this behavior but expected it. Seldanna felt Virion's arms wrap around her back a second later in a returned embrace. It only lasted a few seconds, and Virion broke away first before then suggesting they should get back to the command tent. Neither wanted to be the target of Conall's fury, especially with the war council planning the operation that he hoped would end the war. Seldanna wondered why the sudden need to end the war struck him today. Something felt off about this.

The remaining walk back to the command tent wasn't long, but Virion's subtle limp kept them from walking any faster. By the time they reached the path Radelia where turned, Seldanna could no longer see her fiery braid bouncing with her too-fast gait. It was clear that Radelia knew nothing about Virion's fall or that the rest of her walk to the command tent was alone. Radelia, while fierce, seemed too absorbed in herself at times. Regardless, Seldanna and Virion trudged through the mud. Cresting the small hill outside the command tent, Seldanna thought she heard Virion whimper and wanted to suggest getting a healer's attention but also knew such a comment would draw more of a complaint than necessary. Virion, while a sweet friend, could easily defeat even the stroppiest mules in a competition of stubbornness. Seldanna opened the tent and gently guided Virion through the door with a hand in the small of her back. Only after she fully entered the tent did Seldanna inhale sharply, fully prepared to face the Archmage's ire though she hoped their findings would calm him quickly. Few things bothered him more than tardiness. Aside from the war, it might be his biggest frustration.

"What the hell happened to you two?" Conall asked as the tent flaps closed.

"I slipped and fell in the mud," Virion said, taking her place at the table. She promptly picked up the stack of reports she maintained from the scouts.

Conall, already puffed up like an aggravated bird, deflated hearing Virion's explanation. "Well, if you are both fine, we can continue with our planning. Seldanna, what did you and Radelia discover with the masking spell?"

"We have only good news to report from our testing. Both Virion and Radelia failed to detect either the masking spell or the portal itself through our many rounds of testing."

"That's promising. Do you feel confident that we can send a strike team through a portal into the enemy camp without prematurely revealing their location?"

Radelia started to speak up, but Seldanna cut her off. "I'm certain of nothing, Conall, but Virion *and* Radelia both had the same results. That should be enough to at least build some sound assumptions. It's a reasonable expectation that whatever strike team we send will be fine at least getting there unnoticed."

"Very well. Virion, you mentioned before that we have a narrow time window. How narrow are you talking?" Conall asked.

Virion rifled through her reports but didn't look up from her many papers. "I estimate we have about a half an hour where all five leaders are together in their command tent. I haven't yet determined a true pattern of when they overlap like this, but it's infrequent at best."

"Narrow indeed," Neldor grumbled. "You're sure this is the horse you want pulling your wagon, Archmage?"

Conall, following his best judgement, left his eyes on the map sprawled across the table and spoke instead of acknowledging Neldor's comment. "Who should we send for this?"

Radelia, a fist firmly gripping the tail of her braid, chimed in. "Members for the strike team should come from amongst our strongest Mages. If we don't approach the Children with overwhelming strength, we are sending people to their deaths."

"They don't have to be the strongest on their own though," Seldanna said. "The team's combined strength should match the Children."

"Are you suggesting we sacrifice power for this operation, Seldanna?" Radelia asked, more than a hint of doubt in her voice.

"Not at all. A Mage's casting strength isn't their defining quality."

"You only say that because—"

"Seldanna, since this operation was your idea," Conall said, stepping in before Radelia's claws fully extended, "who do you think should lead the strike team?"

"I have no preference, Conall, but it should be a team effort. Aymon is a strong Mage but lacks the necessary leadership for this, as pained as I am to admit that. Neldor possesses both strength and leadership but his hardheadedness—"

"Let's not go around the table pointing fingers and exposing our weaknesses," Conall suggested as Neldor shifted on his feet.

"I had something I was building toward," Seldanna said. "No single Mage standing around this table is individually capable of leading this operation without failure. This needs to be a team effort regardless of who leads the strike."

"Who do you suggest?" Neldor said, his voice gruffer than normal.

"With the right team, Radelia and I could execute a successful mission."

"I was afraid you would say something like that," the red-haired Mage said.

Conall glanced between Seldanna and Radelia, then lowered his head and gazed at the map again. "Very well. Let's plan this out."

"When is the closest opportunity to launch this assault?" Neldor asked, crossing his arms across his chest, his one eye going back and forth between Seldanna and Conall.

"If the information provided by the scouts is accurate," Virion said, "we should be able to send the team this evening. Our window opens in about an hour."

Beads of sweat formed on Seldanna's forehead, and Radelia tensed, visible even from across the table. "It will probably take us an hour alone to decide who will be on this team. Does that give us enough time to plan this and get everyone involved ready? When would our next opportunity after that?"

Virion rifled through her stack of reports and her eyebrows scrunched. "I don't think we would get the same chance again for another…four days."

"Conall, we haven't even decided what kind of mission this is. We have to make the choice now: are we capturing Lillis and the others or going there to kill?"

"It wouldn't make sense to kill them in their camp. Doing so will only bring unwanted attention to our presence there," Seldanna said. "I think we would have a better chance to end this war with the Children captured, if doing so is safely possible. We do have that dungeon where we can keep them until there is a chance to take them before either of the kings for their trial. We would need to keep them under close watch—"

"You want to keep them *alive* after everything they've caused?" Wollarr asked. Still being new to the war council, he didn't often speak during these sessions.

"They are too dangerous to take before the kings!" Neldor roared. "A trial would be fine if we weren't dealing with a deranged group who wants nothing more than to plunge the world into chaos."

"That's enough!" Conall yelled. "We have too many other tasks to plan and worry about in such a small amount of time. For now, let's say the plan is to capture the enemy leaders if possible. Should we run into issues, lethality may be necessary. Seldanna, Radelia, how do you both sit with this decision?"

The two of them, standing across the table from each other, locked eyes and Conall's gaze darted back and forth between them before they answered in unison, "Agreed, Archmage."

"Very good. Now, how many Mages should we provide your team?" Conall asked.

"Two squads should suffice for this. Any more than that and any strength we gain against the Children doesn't outweigh the loss to our stealth," Radelia suggested. "I know the five of them are strong Mages but catching them off guard should give us some kind of advantage."

Seldanna nodded in agreement. "My only other request before we call our plans finalized is that we should have a second team standing by to assist if necessary."

Conall scratched at the stubble on his chin while he considered their input. Seldanna hadn't noticed before how much grey snuck its way into his facial hair. Was that new? Perhaps the stress of being Archmage were taking their toll on him. Even with this newly discovered touch of age in his face, he kept much of the innocent boyishness that she knew so well. Seldanna worried about him and not only because he seemed tightly wound. With the war going on, no one could possibly be immune to stress. Seldanna kicked herself mentally for not giving those around her more tolerance for that. The many niceties they took for granted before the fighting started five years ago felt like luxuries they couldn't afford now. Laughter, joy, and even the need for rest seemed selfish while others fought and died so close by.

Finally removing his hand from his chin, Conall looked first at Radelia, then Seldanna several seconds later before he spoke. "I won't risk preparing other teams for this mission. We will accept the outcome of this operation, regardless of what happens."

Chapter Eight

...In the Present...

"Forgive me, class. I just need a moment," Seldanna said.

Standing behind the lectern in her classroom, she swallowed to push down the lump in her throat. Until this morning, so many of these specific memories seemed locked behind an unseen barrier that allowed her the briefest occasional sightings but nothing else beyond that. For reasons she couldn't comprehend, something removed that barrier today, and those memories now burst forth like water freed from a beaver's dam. The emotions after she first entered her classroom earlier and seeing the visages of the Children of Chaos seated in chairs now filled by students still overwhelmed her. She turned away from her lectern and her hand trembled as she reached for the glass pitcher of water that sat on a small, circular table right behind her. Each morning, classroom attendants brought these same pitchers of water for all instructing staff and, until today, Seldanna got through her lectures without needing any. Lifting an empty cup from the table, she filled the matching glass as neatly as she could, though she still heard water splatter onto the floor and felt some seep through the toe of her shoe. She ignored this as best she could and sipped at the water briefly before replacing the glass pitcher table and turning back to face her students and Conall again. She did her best not to look at anyone specifically, but she felt herself linger and immediately noticed the unease plastered on Clara's face. The young Elf squirmed in her seat, and her lips parted like she wanted to speak.

"Councilor, I think we should return to the textbooks for the remaining lecture," Conall said from the back of the classroom where he still leaned against the wall by the door.

"We don't want you to push through any discomfort for our sake," Clara added. "Adrian clearly didn't understand the weight of his request."

Seldanna swallowed the small amount of water in her mouth and set the cup down on the small shelf on the inside of the lectern. "I am fine to continue sharing, I just needed to recollect myself. I am experiencing a lot of unexpected and difficult emotions with these memories."

"Councilor, I don't understand what you mean. You lived through these events. Why would the emotions tied to them still be so difficult?" Adrian asked from his seat two rows from the front where he normally sat.

Clara's face twisted with frustration, and she turned around to glower at Adrian. "Trauma isn't an easy thing to simply 'get over', Adr—"

"I'm just wondering. Was the war so long ago that she could forget until now?" he asked, cutting off Clara.

"You're unbelievable, Adrian," Clara huffed before turning her back to him and crossing her arms tightly over her chest.

"Are you really going to insult council—" Ailas chimed in from the end of the row to Adrian's right.

"You have no room to criticize me," Adrian interrupted, "Besides, I'm only trying to understand the situation."

"People died, you mule," Neia said from directly behind Adrian as she flicked the pointed tip of his right ear. "That's the situation."

"You don't have to bring mules into this. They don't deserve association with *him* right now," Ailas scoffed.

"Hey, at least I didn't ask the councilor if she killed anyone in the war," Adrian murmured rubbing the tip of his ear.

Conall took a step away from the back wall and in a mere second cast a simple spell that created two thin blocks of condensed air the length of his hand and smacked them together above the students' heads to create a sharp crack which quieted the classroom and brought their attention toward the headmaster. "That's enough bickering. We are not here to argue amongst ourselves or to judge another on the problematic nature of their questions, while ignoring our own. Ailas,

Neia, and Adrian, you will come to my office after class to further discuss this.”

“Yes, headmaster,” the three said in unison, as they each seemed to try sinking through their chairs to avoid further attention from anyone.

“There’s not enough time left in this lecture period for me to address every question and finish my lesson. Adrian, you asked a fair question about the difficulty of emotions and their connection to even distant memories. It’s hard to explain with my preferred level of detail, but something locked these memories away for a long time in a way that I don’t fully understand myself. They returned earlier this morning and since then more appeared and brought with them their emotions. I feel like I’m in a leaking canoe in the ocean as I struggle to navigate a ravaging storm that brings unrelenting waves,” Seldanna explained before she again grabbed the cup from the small shelf inside the lectern. She took another sip of water and returned the cup to the shelf.

“Councilor, please don’t feel that you need to force yourself through these memories for our sake,” Clara said, the concern written clearly on her face softening for a second.

“Thank you for your consideration, Clara. I will continue though because talking through these memories partially helps with processing their emotions,” Seldanna said before taking a deep breath.

Chapter Nine

...In the Past...

Seldanna sat on the three-legged, wooden stool in her tent, preparing for the upcoming attack against the Children of Chaos. She spent a significant amount of time on the battlefield earlier in the war. Since ascending to her current place on the war council a year prior, she spent her time, not in the trenches, but instead helping to direct the Praetors' efforts. This let her help guide the council's decision making and support the Battlemages in and out of the trenches. Regardless, she rarely slept without thinking of the lives that ended around her through the years of combat. Those lives included ones she directly ended, those who fell around her, and some whose deaths she couldn't prevent. Sitting on her stool now, she couldn't decide which of those would be the hardest to forgive herself for. She couldn't see herself ever forgetting how sticky blood felt while it dried on her hands or the sound of breath leaving a person's lungs for the last time. Screams from wounded Battlemages still rang in her ears, a reminder of how much peace cost. This war consumed too many lives. It felt impossible to know how many more would fade like an extinguished candle before they reached the end of the war. She only hoped that her suggestion brought peace soon.

Like the others on the council, Seldanna commanded a sizable team of Mages. Most of the other council members led teams of five, except Neldor whose team consisted of seven Mages for reasons no one had adequately explained. Each of Seldanna's Mages led their own teams, and this repeated down to the newly graduated Mages coming to the battlefield directly from the Sorcerer's College. Since the war started, the College slightly reduced its standards for a graduated Mage to ensure there were enough Battlemages to continue the fight against the Children of Chaos. That task felt futile at times, but standing idly by would allow the Children to bring about the destruction of, not only Drendil, but elsewhere in the world too.

Rumors circulated through every level on this side of the battlefield that Lillis and the Children intended to bring the world to ruin by any means they could. Fearful whispers in the shadows spoke of failed attempts to summon the Light Eater, a dark deity whose name few wished even to think let alone utter. Seldanna often wondered at the merit behind the rumored mention of Kalathan and if there was any weight to said rumor. Lillis often used hyperbole and Seldanna had no doubt that starting a rumor centered around such a feared being could embolden, radicalize, or panic the Praetors. Even if the Children didn't plan to go half as far as summoning Kalathan into this world, rumors of destruction at a monstrous scale had always circulated and likely carried some truth. Still, Seldanna couldn't fully ignore mentions of Kalathan and a connection with the Children of Chaos.

Seldanna shook her head and refocused on readying for her part in the mission. Preparing for an assault like this felt unusual after she spent so long away from the battlefield. She worried that she might forget something in her preparations and endanger the mission. Her wavy, blonde hair streaked with hints of brown normally stayed down but gathered behind her ears. At most she would make small braids on the sides, but she so rarely tied her hair up. Looking at herself in her small mirror as she considered how to style her hair, she realized she was overthinking and about something that hardly mattered at this moment. She ultimately decided to tie her hair back in a simple bun that would keep it both out of her face and away from anyone who might grab it in whatever fight she faced tonight. The last thing she wanted was to give anyone anything they could use against her.

As she finished putting her hair back, Seldanna concentrated on the face she saw in her mirror. Slight puffiness and darkness around her green-hazel eyes made her appear more tired than she felt. She couldn't think of the last time she slept anywhere near soundly or, at a minimum, through a whole night. Sounds from the battlefield either kept her awake or pulled her from her fitful sleep. She cautiously touched, lifted, and prodded different parts of her face that looked puffier or droopier than she remembered them being before. While only thirty-five years old, she already saw signs of the fight between youth and time's unrelenting, cruel touch. It was such an oddity to her to be fighting not only against the Children but also in her personal war against age. She knew she could only bring about the end to one of these wars, but she wanted to focus on anything other than that reality right now. She opened a small jar that sat on top of her dresser and used the tip of a finger to retrieve a small amount of the cream from within it before dabbing small bits around her face. She closed the jar and set it back before rubbing the cool lotion into her skin. She may not be able to win her war against time, but she could slow it somewhat. She took solace in that.

She stood from the stool and undressed. After removing her muddy clothes, she loosely folded them and placed them on the stool. She opened the middle drawer of her dresser and assessed her options. Her wardrobe, while never fancy, became significantly more spartan since the war started. Simple materials often made of singular, drab colors left her missing her typical array of colors and patterns that she wore before the war. She grabbed a dark blouse and loose, flowing skirt and set them on her bed behind her before closing the drawer. She opened the top drawer and grabbed a pair of dark stockings and a slip. She donned her selected clothes before slipping into and lacing her boots. She made sure the laces were tight enough that she wouldn't lose her boots in the mud but still loose enough to not hurt. It was a delicate balancing act to find the right tension for her laces.

Fully dressed, Seldanna left her tent, stepping into the ever-present downpour joined by a wind so fierce her clothes tried to fly away. Despite the unnaturally overcast sky, the result of a spell the Children cast early in the war, Seldanna knew the sun had descended below the western horizon because the sky turned from a dull slate to a deep charcoal. Lightning flashed through the clouds, the jagged golden bolts providing less than minimal light. The roiling thunder whispered through the dense carpet of clouds that covered the visible sky. Off to the southwest, in the direction of the battlefield, eruptions of spells boomed.

It only took four minutes for Seldanna to reach the small clearing east of their camp where the war council decided the strike team would meet. Radelia and Wollarr already stood in the clearing with Virion and a couple other Mages Seldanna didn't recognize in the deepening darkness as night set in. The group huddled together chatting softly in the darkness. Seldanna approached and stood beside Wollarr, placing her hand gently on his shoulder to silently inform him of her presence. In the enveloping darkness, she could make out few of his features, but she didn't need to see his face to know the apprehension written across it.

"I hope you're ready for this," she said, locking eyes with him.

"There is only so much I can do to prepare. There are too many variables involved here." he replied, his voice low and quiet. "Either we will succeed tonight, or it won't matter long for those of us standing here."

"That's the spirit," Seldanna sighed.

Before Seldanna could ask about the others' whereabouts, Olara, Venali, and Jassin showed up, coming from the north into the clearing. Seldanna counted the faces she could see in the darkness and felt her brow wrinkle when she only counted eight Mages with Virion included. They should have more than this by now.

"Where is everyone else?" she asked.

"Don't worry, they're coming," Radelia answered. "We still have some time before our window even opens."

"How long do we have, Virion?" Seldanna asked. She could feel Radelia's cold eyes on the back of her head.

"All five of them should be in their command tent in about ten minutes. I'll wait for everyone to be here to go over the timeline though."

Seldanna couldn't argue with that rationale. Why would anyone want to waste time repeating themselves. Virion especially wouldn't want to exert more energy socializing than she needed. Seldanna inhaled deeply and attempted to clear the racing thoughts from her mind. Like Wollarr said, either they would succeed tonight or failing wouldn't matter to those preparing for their assault. Even knowing the truth behind his statement, her mind latched onto the idea that they might not succeed, her stomach fluttered, and her hands gripped her crossed arms tight as they stood waiting. She wondered if success meant the same to all of them. Did everyone on the war council picture the same outcome when they envisioned a successful operation? Neldor and Conall likely had different definitions, just as she imagined she and Radelia did. She closed her eyes and calmed herself as best she could while cold, fat raindrops continued falling on her. She could hear as they splattered on her, a sound which she doubted she would ever stop hearing. Wet hair matted to her scalp and forehead and her clothes grew heavy and clung to her like a second skin. She regretted not grabbing her cloak before she left her tent, but most of the rain falling across the battlefield was closer to mist than droplets that splashed into her ear and made her shiver.

The remaining Mages, members of Radelia's squad, arrived momentarily. They approached the group from the same direction from which Seldanna came. Looking around, Seldanna now counted twelve Mages in the clearing aside from Virion. With everyone now gathered in the clearing, additional footsteps approached from the east behind Radelia. Conall and Neldor materialized from the gloom beyond the gathered Mages, their presence a surprise. Conall walked into the center of the group while Neldor stood at the edge, his grim expression hovering over Radelia's right shoulder. Conall looked into the faces of each Mage around him before he started speaking. He lingered for a second longer when he looked at both Radelia and Seldanna.

"Thank you all for coming tonight. I have no doubt that Seldanna and Radelia explained the gravity of this situation. We'll open the portal that will send you to face our enemies, but before that, I want to allow an opportunity for anyone feeling hesitant about what may happen to step away now with no repercussions," he said. After several seconds with no one moving, he continued. "Very well. Our historians will remember each of you fondly regardless of how this night plays out. Virion, can you please explain your part of this?"

"Of course, Archmage," she said wringing her hands together. "We have a small window of time where we can most likely guarantee the success of this operation. From the information the scouts have provided, you should fully expect all five Children of Chaos leaders to be in their command tent when you arrive. Two Mages are always standing guard outside their tent. These two, at a minimum, will hear whatever commotion happens inside the tent. I don't want to tell anyone how to run their missions, but dealing with the guards first will benefit everyone."

"Our goal is to capture the Dark Mages, but should they choose to respond with violence, don't be afraid to respond accordingly. Reach whatever solution the situation allows," Conall added, his wording intentionally vague. "Radelia and Seldanna, iron out whatever specifics you need to here."

"We need someone to deal with the guards outside the tent," Seldanna said.

"Venali and I can do that," Wollarr volunteered. Venali nodded her agreement.

"Virion, do we know when these guards change out?" Seldanna asked.

"Dawn and dusk roughly. You shouldn't have any interruptions here," she said.

"Do we want to split ourselves into two teams and pinch the Children? Seldanna since this was your idea, I'll let you decide," Radelia said.

"Once the guards are handled, Wollarr and Venali can enter from the front of the tent and close off any escape route they would have there."

"What's the plan then?" Radelia asked.

"We'll burn through the back of their tent while masking the spell. That should catch them off guard. Whatever happens after that will depend on how they react," she replied, her voice staying smoother than she expected.

"That's about what I figured we should do," Radelia said.

"Very well. We will get the portal made. Allfather guide you all," Conall said.

Neldor and Conall cast a portal and masking spell together, and a shimmering doorway opened behind Jassin and the others on the north side of the huddle. Radelia and Seldanna broke from the group first and walked toward the doorway that flickered in the air. Radelia's face showed less emotion than a stone as she locked eyes with Seldanna. They nodded at each other and stepped through the portal in tandem with Radelia in front, followed by the rest of the team.

Chapter Ten

Portal spells were incredibly useful for improving transportation, whether for a single person, a group, or even supply wagons, and there was not a Mage alive who would dispute that. Of course, like everything else, some serious limitations existed for these, just the same as with most spells. The biggest drawback for the traveler's safety was that when opening a portal, the caster needed to have a painstakingly clear mental image of the destination, otherwise the results could be chaotic at best. Cautionary tales from the early days of learning the art of spellcasting told of two dozen bystanders who went missing the day Mages discovered portals. The records written by Master Fylson and his apprentice Kieran mentioned nothing about ever learning the whereabouts of those travelers, but Seldanna doubted anyone found them. The only hope she and anyone else had was that wherever they ended up after stepping through the portal was at least livable. She questioned whether Master Fylson or Kieran were honest with those who they convinced to take part in their experiments. Right now, that hardly mattered.

Creating the spell also physically taxed the Mage, but that held true for all spells. Holding a spell open also took a toll on the caster. Ensuring a proper destination for the portal and preserving your strength were the only real drawbacks to account for with portals. Anyone stepping through a portal needed to put a great deal of trust in whoever opened it to have gotten the destination correct. On the battlefield, some Mages used portals to deflect spells away and, in those moments, where the portals opened didn't matter as much.

Seldanna never worried about where a portal might take her, but she disliked how it felt when she stepped through the cold, viscous surface. In the century that passed since the discovery of this spell, it baffled her that no one figured out a way to cast them that might remove the slick jelly. Whenever she stepped through a portal, the surface left her skin prickled like a freshly plucked chicken and colder than if she had jumped into the lake near her childhood home on the morning of the winter solstice. She welcomed neither sensation right now with the unrelenting rain ensuring she stayed consistently drenched. Safely on the other side of the portal, she opened her eyes and wiped her hand down her face. She always expected there would be residue on her face but was surprised every time there was none.

After exiting the portal, Seldanna and Radelia stepped to the side while the rest of the strike team filed through the doorway Conall and Neldor made back in the clearing. After the last person exited, the shimmering doorway that waved like air above a campfire snapped shut in the bizarre, soundless way portals closed. Seldanna felt her heartbeat quicken as the reality of their isolation firmly set in around her. The darkness of night seemed denser here on the outskirts of the Children's camp. Seldanna looked around to take in their surroundings. She needed a clear understanding of her whereabouts as that helped calm her nerves when facing uncertainties. Grounding herself in fact and reality was better for everyone than allowing fear and anxieties to run amok. A chill ran up her spine as she imagined a withered, decaying hand reaching for her from somewhere beyond this world. She wanted to do anything she could to keep those long, bony fingers from even gripping her. She shook her head and focused on her surroundings.

Twenty steps to her left stood a large, dark tent like those in the Praetors' own camp. To her right stretched an expanse of gently rolling hills that she knew to be the western Arngan Fields. Far off in the distance, stretched a road beyond where her eyes could see even without the blanket of clouds impeding the moonlight. That road served as the far western edge of the Fields which stretched east to the foothills of the Ash Mountains behind her where the Dwarves had long ago established their kingdom of unseen mines and secluded themselves from the surface races. No matter the severity of a squabble the humans and Elves faced, the Dwarves seemed only interested in finding and wrenching whatever precious materials they could from the planet's bowels. For the better part of two centuries, the Dwarves thrived almost entirely underground. Only once in her life had Seldanna seen a Dwarf who served as a traveling merchant for their mine colonies.

Going south along the road eventually led to Shemont, the capital of the humans' half of the kingdom. Following the same road north first led to the Sorcerer's College before later arriving at Anselin, the Elven capital. Only a handful of trees obstructed the landscape, and those she could barely see were solitary giants who supplied shade to animals and people alike as they traversed Arngan Fields. Seldanna let her thoughts dwell on the idea of traveling the countryside before the war started but finally wrangled her thoughts away from her surroundings and returned to the task at hand. Even before stepping through the portal, their miniscule window of time started closing, and they couldn't afford to let this opportunity slip through their fingers. They had to finish this before any of the Children of Chaos left their command tent.

Looking back over toward the strike team, a spark of hope flashed briefly within her. A faint flicker of light that fought valiantly against the imposing darkness brought by despair. The end of the war could be well within their grasp. A brief, undoubtedly disastrous hurdle stood between the Praetors and that possibility. She looked to her left, her eyes seeking the ever-familiar tightly braided copper hair. She quickly found what she sought even in the stormy, evening gloom. Radelia apparently took no time grounding herself in her surroundings and now spun her right hand in a tight circle above her shoulder signaling for the group to move out. Wollarr and Venali walked up to her and a brief, low conversation Seldanna couldn't hear before Radelia turned slightly to her right to lock eyes with Seldanna. Her jade-green eyes normally overflowed with grit and determination but now showed the faintest hint of uncertainty. Seldanna, unsure what Radelia wanted from her, nodded to her counterpart hoping it would instill some encouragement in her. Instead, Radelia turned back to the other two and passed some sort of directions on to Wollarr and Venali. The two Mages nodded then crept off into the darkness that gathered at the left side of the larger tent. Once beside the tent, Wollarr looked back and raised his thumb. Even without being privy to the previous conversation, Seldanna knew they were in position. Time for the rest of the team to do the same.

Seldanna and Radelia quietly approached the back of the tent and the rest of the strike team gathered behind them. Seldanna closed her eyes briefly and inhaled deeply before stretching her fingers and clenching her fists. Her knuckles crackled and a moment later Radelia pointed to the back of the Children's tent and motioned her hands in a rectangle as if to signal she was ready for them to go through. Seldanna started a spell that Radelia masked with another. As they learned from their testing with Virion earlier, this would keep the Children from sensing these spells and would preserve the element of surprise for as long as possible. Seldanna hovered her spell over the canvas panel of the tent for a second. Her heart fluttered. She proposed this plan. The war council approved it. Here she stood behind the tent where Virion and her scouts fervently believed they would find the Children of Chaos. If the strike team could trust the scouts' reported information, and Virion's track record for accuracy was nearly immaculate, Lillis, Aska, Troy, Celeste, and Serena waited on the other side of this thin, fabric wall. Seldanna knew she was stalling but didn't know how to stop doing so or why she hesitated even for just the briefest moment. She swallowed the lump forming in her throat.

"Allfather guide us," she breathed. A spiderweb of golden lightning zapped through the clouds overhead and a drumroll of thunder rumbled as Seldanna pushed her spell fully into the fabric tent wall. A swarm of fluttering butterfly wings erupted in her stomach as the white-hot strings of fire traced their way along the canvas and burned open a doorway large enough in the tent for three members of the strike team to enter at once.

Chapter Eleven

It only took a moment. Seldanna stared into the Children's tent as the singed tatters of cloth fell to the ground. Her eyes widened as the five of them stopped where they stood and gazed back at her through the hole she made. She felt like this moment stretched for an eternity, a mask of unbroken but reluctant tranquility falling over the scene. Seldanna and Radelia stood at the edge of the Children's tent with Eliyen between them. A large, dark table with six chairs around it took up a large amount of space in the middle of the tent. Lillis stood between the table and the closed door flaps at the other end of the tent. Troy, his large frame making him forever impossible to miss, sat in a chair to Lillis's right, an empty chair between the two of them. He was both tall and muscular, his stature reminding Seldanna of a bull moose roaming the most northern woods in Drendil. The empty chair being slightly larger and more detailed than the others, it must have been the chair Lillis used to control their side of the battlefield. Celeste and Serena sat on Seldanna's side of the table, and they both looked over their shoulders to see what caused the commotion and warped the face of their leader into a deepening scowl. Aska sat at the end of the table closest to Radelia, a look of utter disbelief etched on her face like a name carved into a headstone.

Seldanna never expected ever to see these five again since the Betrayal which sparked the war. She never considered herself a romantic, but she couldn't deny that Troy alone caused a complex level of emotions to swirl within her. He made her insides flutter like she was a schoolgirl interacting with her first crush. In some ways, that's exactly what she had been while they studied at the College together. In this moment when the Children and the strike team simply stood there staring at each other, she hardly recognized him. Everything about him seemed different, his entire countenance changed. Each looked utterly different than before. Dark bands surrounded their sunken eyes like something started sucking their souls from them near the start of the war. Their faces all looked gaunt, and their cheeks hollow.

Lillis looked the least changed, but whatever had touched one of them firmly grasped them all. Seeing them again, closer than at the Betrayal, Seldanna knew the source of their powers sapped life from them. How could they justify continuing with this vampiric exchange of power? She hoped that someday they could see and step away from this path they chose. All the death and destruction they caused never negated her desire to see them return from this chosen chaos to something closer to normalcy. She doubted any others on the war council wanted that for these five wayward Mages and any they convinced to join their ranks. Even if she stood alone in her desire for them to return, she would hope for that outcome regardless.

The briefest moment of tenuous peace shattered like a mirror after a child throws a rock at the reflective surface. An echoing roar emerged from both Lillis and Troy as he stood from his chair. Radelia and Eliyen stepped to their left and readied spells. Seldanna moved to her right, wanting to make room for the rest of the team to enter the already crowded tent. Esta and Amerie filled the gap between Seldanna and Eliyen. In the same instant that they move forward, a pillar of fire erupted from the ground engulfing them completely. Seldanna couldn't hear their screams over the sound of the fire burning away flesh. Lillis and the Children wasted little time to show their true colors. Perhaps Lillis was beyond redemption, but one of the others surely had a chance. Seldanna refused to give up hope.

Trying to push away the sizzling of burning flesh, and the accompanying smell, Seldanna cast a spell that shoved a wall of hardened air forward toward Lillis, Troy, and Celeste, the latter of whom was still standing from her chair. She hoped that in doing this, she could at least break their concentration so someone else could cut them off from their Magic. It wouldn't fully subdue them, but a Mage unable to cast spells would at least be easier to deal with. In a physical battle, Troy would pose the most difficult fight. Behind and to her right, Seldanna heard the next canvas tent panel sizzle as the rest of the strike team burned another entrance into the tent. As that panel fell to the floor, Seldanna's spell struck the Children, knocking first Celeste out of her chair and to the ground before next contacting Troy and finally Lillis. Troy jostled slightly but otherwise remained unmoved. Lillis staggered back a step. Serena also toppled, an unintended target of the blast, and landed face first on the tent floor under the table. Seldanna winced internally seeing how close Serena's head came to striking the edge of the table.

Seldanna had only the briefest moment to celebrate before the enraged Troy summoned his entire might and he slammed his fists into the table. She reeled at the sight of such a formerly gentle person having so much rage that he would even consider slamming his fists let alone following through. Seldanna stepped forward before a blast of air from her left slammed into her, knocking her backwards. Before she could even see who cast the spell, she found herself tumbling into the thick mud. As she left the tent, lightning crackled where she previously stood. The softness of the ground smeared beneath her, and a new wave of chills washed over her once she stopped moving and settled in the mud. She heard more spells erupting from within the tent and moved to her feet, but the world jolted around her. Even with her best efforts she was only able to loll over onto her side a moment before her stomach revolted and forcefully emptied itself onto the ground. Her body felt confused with one side still covered by the coldness of the mud and now feeling warmth on her chest as her vomit sloshed back into herself.

The world spun around her, and she tried to free herself from the mud. Moving as fast as she could manage, she got to her knees, supported by her hands as they now sank into the ground. The muck squished between her fingers and covered the back of her hands in an instant. She felt the cold and damp halfway between her wrist and elbow before she stopped sinking. Her stomach lurched again, and she dry heaved before a massive hand gripped her neck and jerked her from the ground. Before she fully understood her situation, she was staring into Troy's shrouded face and his eyes that burned with a deep rage. His pale blue eyes once overflowed with care for those around him, but now she saw only death and pain there instead.

Pressure on her neck grew stronger and Seldanna knew she had to act fast. She couldn't let this happen. *Wouldn't* let him be what ended her life. Her hands clawed at his wrist and fingers trying to break his grasp as it still tightened. Her vision blurred and she blinked away the tears flooding her eyes. Darkness formed around the edges of her vision, closing in toward the center. She could only see his face. She reached for his face with her right hand, hoping she could break him from his bloodlust. She reached but touched nothing but air. Desperately she gasped, needing whatever air she could get into her lungs. Her chest burned. Her vision darkened further, everything now hidden. The pressure remained steady on her neck and her feet dangled beneath her, the ground an unknown distance beneath her. Sound faded from her ears, and in a moment, she floated on a sea of nothingness. Everything simply ceased. Peace surrounded her, calm amid the storm.

She began to embrace the frail sense of tranquility she faced, when suddenly she knew she was falling. Sound returned, first distant and soft then growing louder, and breath rushed into her lungs, a sweet relief that also brought a burning pain. She coughed violently as air filled her lungs. Seldanna found herself back in the mud outside of the Children's command tent. Everything came screaming back to her. The chill of the mud as it tried to swallow her whole as if she were a rat found by a snake, the crackling sounds of the distant battlefield, groans and grunts of nearby fighting, the acrid smell of burnt flesh that no longer make her stomach churn but instead reminded her of her mother's kitchen disasters, and the continued struggle of the strike team against the Children. When her vision finally returned, she blinked repeatedly and looked around at the fight between the Children and the strike team.

The smoldering remains of Esta and Amerie still lay on the floor of the Children's tent while the rest of the strike team continued their fight. Three other Mages also fell from the start, but Seldanna couldn't see who they were as every blink forced the stars and blurs that filled her vision to dance around. Troy no longer stood before her and instead fought both Wollarr and Almar, the human Mage from Radelia's squad. Even in the darkness, Seldanna saw blood streaming down the right side of Troy's face from his hairline, and blood matted his hair on the back of his head. Eliyen stood behind Aska, holding onto the shorter Mage with all her might. Aska kicked her legs and writhed as she tried to break free from her captor's grasp. Radelia cast a spell that slammed into Lillis to break her from her Magic. Venali and Eldrin cornered Celeste, who screamed as she threw a spell that knocked Eldrin's feet out from under him. A sharp crack sounded as his chin contacted the ground when he landed. Blood gushed from his mouth accompanied by a slightly muffled yowl. Venali took advantage of Celeste focusing too long on the wounded Eldrin and closed the gap between them. With one swift movement, Venali thrust her right arm forward and wrapped it around the ashen-haired Mage's neck and tucked Celeste's head firmly under her arm. Celeste squawked in surprise as Venali grabbed her, but the sound cut short, replaced with a faint grunt when Venali planted a well-aimed left hook in her ribs.

Seldanna slowly started getting back to her feet but had to stop in the process to catch her breath. By the time she finally got to her feet, Eldrin stopped moving, though blood still came from his now-open mouth as he lay on the ground. Lillis and Radelia closed the gap between them and were fighting more aggressively with fewer spells. Troy spun on his heels and threw a punch which caught Almar squarely in the left cheek. Bones crunched from the force of the blow, and Almar crumpled to the ground like a discarded sack of potatoes. Wollarr wasted no time in retaliating and shoved his boot into the side of Troy's extended knee. Seldanna heard a sickening crunch and the Elven behemoth roared in agony before he buckled and clutched at his knee. As Tory dropped to the ground, Wollarr cast a spell that bound Troy in a net of transparent, fibrous strands stronger than the steel used to forge swords throughout the continent. Troy continued his bellowing until Wollarr cast another spell that gagged Troy. Even in his current state, Troy writhed on the ground as he tried to break free. Rage burned in his eyes.

Wollarr panted heavily and doubled over and gasped repeatedly before he looked at Almar then Seldanna. "I'm so glad we got to you in time. Are you alright, Sel?"

Many people throughout her life had asked that question before, and her normal answers ranging from vague dismissal to her genuine feelings. In this moment, she couldn't think of the words to form, and she felt numb more than anything. She took stock of herself so she could form an answer for Wollarr's question. She wasn't bleeding anywhere that she could see, and she was able to stand. Her neck hurt but given her situation moments before, she could understand that sensation. She looked down at Troy laying in the mud and her vomit hoping she would see a repentant look on his face, but she only saw the same rage barely concealed by an ocean of pain. Even now, he refused to break him from this path of evil he chose. Perhaps he and the others truly were beyond return. Thinking that may be possible, internally voicing an idea she didn't want to admit, hurt more than anything.

Not wanting to dwell on that thought, she brought her attention back to the fading fight inside the tent. Eliyen, who still clung tightly to the struggling Aska, was on the ground atop the once-pretty Mage who was a frequent source of envy for Seldanna and others. Seldanna would have done much to have a complexion that didn't redden with a burn after two seconds in the sun only to return to its original pastiness once healed. Nearby, Radelia and Venali, now finished dealing with Celeste, bound an unconscious Lillis in a spell like what Wollarr used earlier on Troy. Seldanna looked around frantically trying to find Serena but soon saw her on the ground under Malon and Gaelin who must have fallen earlier when Troy…

"Seldanna? Don't move, something's wrong," Wollarr said, taking a shaky step and reaching his hands toward her.

His voice jostled her attention back to herself and after a moment trying to form words only to feel unbearable pain in her neck, she shook her head gently. Even that subtle movement hurt her neck. Wollarr took another step closer and raised his hands to her face as he closed the gap between them. Seldanna flinched and backed away as his hands neared her face but finally let him touch her. His hands were soft and warm against her mud-caked face. In a moment his palms chilled, and her breath caught from the temperature change. She closed her eyes when the healing spell started and braced herself against the icy rush that swept through her like flood waters that crashed through a valley after snow melted during the spring thaw. She gasped as a second wave of cold swept through right after the first with no time between them to breathe. Her hands and legs quivered as this frigid wave tore through her, and in the next moment it all stopped when Wollarr's warming hands left her face. Seldanna opened her eyes and saw the fading concern on Wollarr's face.

"Thank you. I didn't think I would survive that," she said, with a touch of hoarseness still straining her voice.

"You're welcome," he replied. "We should check on the others. I think we've taken care of everything we can here."

Seldanna stepped toward Almar and knelt at his side, touching her fingers gently against his neck. "He's still alive but will need a healer soon or that may change." Wollarr started to approach but Seldanna stopped him. "This might drain your strength too much. We still need to get back. Let me see what I can do."

"You're right. I will start preparing for our return," he said before looking around at the remnants of the chaos from their fight with the Children. "I expected resistance but nothing like this. I truly hope this ends the war. I don't want to see how the others in this camp retaliate when they learn what happened here. Allfather help us."

Seldanna cast a simple healing spell to stabilize Almar's injuries, stood, waited for the dizziness that struck her to subside, and walked toward the tent where the rest of the fight happened. Radelia stood behind the table panting, sweat dripping down her face, finally finished with her struggle against Lillis. She looked at Seldanna and puffed out her cheeks before forcing air through pursed lips. Her left cheek now sported fresh red and puffy scratch marks. Lillis must have fought as much as possible before Radelia subdued her. As much as it pained her, Seldanna looked to her left at the charred remains of Esta and Amerie; tendrils of smoke still rose from them. Their contorted bodies stilled long ago, but she wondered how long they suffered before they died. Eliyen, not far from the burnt bodies, clutched her side where blood soaked through her clothes. When did she get injured? So much must have happened while Troy had her lifted off the ground. Wollarr stepped into the tent and rushed toward Eliyen before kneeling next to her and moving her hand away from her wound. She winced loudly when he started the healing spell. It lasted five seconds, so Seldanna knew he was only doing initial triage so she wouldn't worsen before she could get to a proper healer. Once finished with Eliyen, Wollarr grabbed the bound Aska from next to her and carried her out of the tent, placing her on the ground next to Troy. She struggled much less compared to Troy who still fought against his bindings.

"Seldanna, we need to get out of here before any others shows up. We've caused more than a small ruckus, and not one of us got through this unscathed. If we have any others show up, we won't get back alive," Radelia said, her terse voice breaking Seldanna's concentration from surveying the aftermath.

"Yes, let's do that. How many of them did we capture?"

"I think all of them."

"Conall should be pleased," Seldanna replied.

"You should be as well. This plan was your idea after all," Radelia said. "Even if we only captured one of them, I would consider this a success."

"How many of us are left?" Wollarr asked standing beside Seldanna. "I don't think there are enough of us to carry the Children and our casualties back in one trip."

"I will take care of that," Radelia said, as she cast a spell that compressed water and air together to form a makeshift sledge. "Let's gather those we can and get them on here."

"Those we can?" Eliyen asked as she stood. "You can't seriously consider leaving anyone behind."

"We may have to leave our dead behind." Radelia grunted, lifting Eldrin by the armpits to place him on the sledge. Wollarr helped place him the rest of the way, and Radelia wiped sweat from her face before answering. "It's not a decision I come to lightly, but we need to leave here soon."

"We can't leave them here for the Children to defile their bodies however they want," Eliyen said, her voice breaking. "We lost good Mages here. They deserve better than that fate."

"Let's not bicker about this," Radelia said.

"I'm not *bickering*, I'm trying to make sure our fallen get the respect they deserve for the sacrifice they—" Eliyen started.

"This is a difficult situation for everyone here," Seldanna said.

Wollarr gently lowered Almar onto the sledge Radelia created. "His heartbeat is fading. We need to get him to a healer soon or we'll lose him."

"Yes, let's get him to a healer so Radelia can't choose to leave him behind."

"Eliyen, we can debate the ethics of this later. Check for other survivors and get them here. Seldanna, let's get the Children through a portal so Conall and Neldor can deal with moving them how they wish. I want as little to do with them as possible," Radelia said, opening a portal and grabbing Aska off the ground before stepping through.

Seldanna looked to Eliyen briefly and tried to make her face as sympathetic as possible before looking to her right for where she saw Serena. Virion's former wife was unconscious, trapped beneath a pile of downed Mages. Seldanna touched the necks and wrists of her comrades checking for heartbeats, then moved people out of the way so she could retrieve Serena from the ground. She crossed paths with Radelia on her way to the portal and held her breath as she stepped through the wavering doorway, expecting the cold, viscous fluid to wash over her as she approached. She dared not lock eyes with Eliyen as she chose to grab a traitor instead of one of their own. Tensions were already high enough; she didn't want to add any fuel to the fire.

Chapter Twelve

Seldanna had never stepped through a portal so many times in such a short period and wished a similar situation never arose. She wondered how long it would take for her skin to release the prickles that covered her whole body. It took three trips through the portal to get all the Children out of their camp. Radelia took Aska and Celeste and Seldanna took Serena and Lillis. Wollarr helped to carry Troy which was still difficult even with three people. Eliyen made a separate sledge for those who died but couldn't retrieve Esta or Amerie from where they fell. She tried but threw up after trying to lift them and breaking a chunk of charred flesh from the first body she grabbed. There was nothing identifiable between the two, and there was no way of knowing if she had grabbed Esta or Amerie. Seldanna's stomach lurched simply thinking of that moment again, much the same as watching it happen. She doubted anyone could easily forget such a traumatic moment.

Shaking the memory free from her mind, Seldanna grabbed the front of Radelia's sledge which now only carried the Praetors' wounded. Wollarr grabbed the back and Radelia stood across from Seldanna. As it picked up speed, Radelia and Seldanna let go of the sides of the sledge and let Wollarr push it through the portal on his own. He stepped through and Seldanna approached, with Radelia not far behind her. Seldanna stopped and turned to make sure they weren't leaving anyone behind before she strode through the portal one final time. The cold surface passed over her skin again before she found herself back in the clearing on the outskirts of their camp where Conall, Neldor, and Virion saw them off at the start of this do-or-die mission.

While they fought the Children, Virion left the clearing. Conall and Neldor gathered their quarry into an uncovered wagon with a single horse hitched at the front, its tail swishing back and forth in the rain. The bench at the front of the wagon was empty, but it seemed wide enough room to fit two people comfortably. Seldanna walked toward the wagon as Conall placed Celeste into the back a moment before Neldor heaved Aska to the pile of captives. Conall seemed much gentler with Celeste, setting her onto the wagon before pushing her further into the bed. Neldor tossed Aska from his shoulder as if she were nothing more than a sack of root vegetables he bought at the market.

"I know she's the enemy, Neldor, but you could at least treat her with even just a crumb of respect," Seldanna said as she approached.

"Why would I waste my energy on such a useless notion?" he grumbled, not bothering to look at Seldanna as he turned away from the wagon.

"I didn't think it was possible for you to be any more of an ass, but I will admit when I'm wrong," she said, her fists clenching at her sides.

"Seldanna, you need to understand that this is war. Gentility and manners flew out the window when these animals," he said pointing toward the now-filled wagon, "started this shit. The fact that they're alive right now is more than they deserve."

"You talk to me about what war is as if I wasn't fighting in the trenches—"

"Do you not see my missing—" he started.

"That's enough, both of you!" Conall's voice was firm but level. "We are so close to stopping all this death and fighting. Everyone standing here right now has made untold sacrifices to bring us to this point. Digging into ourselves won't solve any of our problems."

"You are all soft. This is a fucking war and you're worried about how I treat a traitorous Dark Mage?" Neldor growled.

"Try to hide your feelings better, Neldor," Conall said. "Seldanna, get in the wagon."

"Why would I do that?" she asked.

"You came up with this idea, so you're coming with me."

"Where are we going?" The indignation in her voice deflated into reluctance.

"Taking them to the dungeon. I'm not sure what we will do from there, but we can figure that out later," Conall answered.

Seldanna walked along the right side of the wagon and climbed into the seat. The mud on her boots and the wet wood of the ladder together felt slick, so she moved slowly to make sure she didn't slip. Despite her efforts, her right foot skidded off the flat rung and threatened to throw her to the ground. Her left foot stayed planted on the next step, and she kept her hands on the rail easily. Conall seemed not to notice as he settled onto the bench, but he waited until she seated herself before he grabbed the horse's reins and snapped them. The wagon lurched briefly as the horse started walking but settled soon when their speed maintained. Conall guided the horse and wagon through the clearing north to a road that meandered along the outside of the camp. Seldanna couldn't see much beyond the horse and turned to keep an eye on the captives. Conall noticed and glanced over his shoulder briefly before locking his eyes on the road again.

"We should reach the dungeon by midmorning," Conall said. Seldanna said nothing and continued watching the Children in the back of the wagon. "We could use a portal to take us there faster, but I fear the Children may have scouts watching our camp."

Chapter Thirteen

How much longer until we arrive, Conall?" Seldanna asked, her jaw crackling from a large, drawn-out yawn.

She normally kept her patience well, but riding on the wagon for such a long time taxed her more than she expected. With a quick glance at the Archmage she saw fatigue plastered on his face too. Were they riding through a forest under most other circumstances, she would likely be unphased by how long it took, but the presence of the Children of Chaos in the back of the wagon concerned her greatly. Sitting on the bench beside Conall, Seldanna half-turned to keep an eye on their cargo. Each of the Dark Mages were bound and gagged using the same spell Wollarr used on Troy outside of their command tent. Troy no longer struggled against his bonds, something which, at first, brought Seldanna some comfort but now worried her. She wondered if he was still conscious in the back or if perhaps the pain from his injuries finally overwhelmed him. Serena and Lillis seemed to be the only two conscious now, and Serena only recently woke up after the fight. Lillis stared at the back of Conall's head, not once breaking her concentration from him. Seldanna saw nothing but hatred burning in her eyes.

"We're close," Conall said, wiping one hand down his face and keeping the other on the reins. "The building should be in view soon."

Seldanna turned back around to briefly admire the scenery ahead of the wagon. The forest that surrounded them felt unnaturally calm. She saw no signs of small animals scurrying along the ground or in the trees. She heard birds chittering far from the wagon but saw no sign of them as they rolled down the rarely used, overgrown track in the forest. Sunlight streamed through the treetops and her eyes burned even in the filtered light. So many on the battlefield spent much of the past few years in artificial darkness, or at most among candle or lantern light, that Seldanna wondered what the lasting consequences would be for war survivors.

She felt thankful that the rain stopped before they reached the edge of the forest. With the sun rising, and with it the temperature, Seldanna was glad that her clothes dried off. Conall no longer pulled at his robes either, a clear sign he also appreciated being dry. Why he chose to wear his robes through the war was beyond her. Some of the other Battlemages chose the same early on, but most switched away from them during the war. Seldanna ran her fingers through her hair and was pleased to find it no longer felt damp. She wished she didn't have to appreciate dry hair so much.

"Have you thought about what we'll do when we arrive?" Seldanna asked, turning back to look at the Children in the back of the wagon.

"We can discuss that later," Conall answered, launching them back into silence. "At the very least, we shouldn't discuss our plan in front of them."

"So, you're unsure?" Seldanna asked.

"You don't have to sound so arrogant about being right."

"I meant no offense, Conall."

"Seldanna, that was a joke."

"Oh," Seldanna said, heat flooding into her cheeks, "right…"

Through a gap that formed in the trees, Seldanna caught her first glimpses of a decrepit, abandoned building with vines covering one side as nature fought to reclaim what man once built long ago. Weathered, grey stone peeked through the forest's green foliage, a stark contrast between the two. The track the wagon followed, two ruts cutting their way through thick, overgrown grass and underbrush, continued straight as far as she could see, but a branch formed in the path that turned sharply right toward the structure. Within a couple minutes they reached this fork in the path, and it wasn't long after that when Conall stopped the horse and climbed off the bench. Seldanna also left the wagon and walked around the right side and waited at the back while Conall approached the weathered, moss-covered stairs to open the outer door to the building. She heard the lock disengage a moment before the hinges moaned when the door opened. With that task accomplished, Conall returned to the wagon. Seldanna thought she saw Conall shudder as he made his way down the stairs, but it happened so fast and faded just as quickly that she chalked it up to her tired delirium.

"Ever been here before?" Conall asked as he climbed the short ladder into the wagon.

"I haven't, but I heard that it existed some time ago. I hoped I would never see it."

"Right. This isn't our best-kept secret," Conall admitted. "Of course, I would prefer not to even continue maintaining the dungeon any longer, but for right now it serves its purpose. As a warning, once you walk through that door, the warding spells will cut you off from your Magic until you leave. It's the worse sensation I've ever felt, and it's not one that gets less uncomfortable the longer you are here or the more you experience it. Let me know if it becomes too much for you. Would rather not have you more perturbed than necessary if I can avoid that."

"I appreciate that. I'll let you know if anything gets to be too much."

"Glad to hear you don't have any questions about the ward," Conall said.

"How are we going to do this?" Seldanna asked, motioning at the wagon's occupants in what she hoped would be a successful attempt at changing the subject.

"Well, I hadn't thought that far ahead. I suppose we probably need some assistance with this, don't we. I doubt we'll be able to get Troy downstairs without at least another person or spells. We should be able to manage with the others, right?"

"Sure. We can get the ladies situated first. I'll take Aska, Celeste, and Serena on my own. If you want to grab Lillis, I'll take Aska and follow you into the dungeon."

"If you're fine with this plan, we can certainly do that," Conall said as he helped situate Aska on Seldanna's shoulders before he exited the wagon and picked up Lillis. "While you are carrying the other two, I can recruit some help from the camp."

"Let's get to it then," Seldanna suggested. She almost wanted to comment on the gentility to how he carried his counterpart from the other side of the battlefield, especially compared to how Neldor handled the situation earlier. Rather than starting any tiffs, she swallowed her sarcasm and took her first step toward the dungeon with Aska across her shoulders.

She followed behind Conall as he walked up the stairs and through the square-topped door made from iron bars and bands covered in decades of rust. Above the door was a half-circle window with half of the panes of glass missing, and on either side were narrow slits through the stone façade. Inside the dungeon was dim and stale, as Seldanna would have expected for a building that, in this century, only saw occasional, short-term use. The only source of light seemed to be sunlight coming through a hole in the ceiling and the broken, vine-covered windows set in the back wall. While the temperature outside was warm, as happened when spring transitioned to summer, inside felt frigid. She half expected to see her breath form a cloud of mist before her face as she exhaled. The change of temperature made her chest feel like she was wearing too tight of a corset for a formal dinner with her mother. Seldanna always dreaded those dinners, but also missed the simpler time in her life when wearing formal attire or sitting still for Selona to meticulously brush, tease, and shape her hair were the worst of her concerns. She would sacrifice much in her current life for that to still be the case. That thought firmed itself in her mind as she shifted Aska's weight across her shoulders and shakily started down the stairs behind Conall. She moved from one step to the next as gingerly as she could, despite her legs trembling as she descended the stairs.

She reached a landing and turned right before taking another step down to a second, lower landing. Another right turn and she saw yet another set of stairs darker than those she just descended. Flickers of faint, orange light danced beyond the bottom of the stairs, and Seldanna found herself thankful to have even that much light. Curiosity struck her, and she wondered for quite some time why light existed in this empty building, but she disregarded the thought after she reached the third step down and needed to concentrate more on her descent. She reached the bottom where she found herself in a small room furnished with a single wooden table with three spartan chairs placed casually around it. To her left and right were wooden doors bound with rusted iron fittings. Conall stood at the door to the right while he worked on inserting the key into the lock and holding onto Lillis at the same time. Seldanna stood behind Conall and did her best not to pant like a dog in the full summer sun while streams of sweat poured down her face. Anger flared inside her as she saw Conall hadn't even broken a sweat coming down the stairs. He somehow also didn't have the same trembling leg problems she did and that also annoyed her. Thankfully, he soon had the door unlocked and opened before motioning Seldanna through the doorway ahead of him with a tilt of his head.

On the other side of the door was a room with a single walkway and four cells on each side. Iron bars and stone walls separated the single room into smaller spaces, each meant to hold a prisoner for however long they stayed here. Seldanna took two steps into the room and shuffled to the side so Conall could get around her. He walked to the far end of the room and opened the door on the right before stepping in and placing Lillis on the ground. He stepped backwards out of her cell and closed the door before setting the lock. He motioned to the space across the walkway from Lillis's cell and Seldanna placed Aska on the floor. Conall closed the door once Seldanna backed out of the small space and again set the lock. She took a moment to look through the iron bars at both prisoners before taking a deep breath and walking out of the cell room behind Conall. Out of the room, he closed the wooden door and waved his arms before him as if he were opening the floor to comments on a tour he gave of the College's dungeon.

"We can't use our Magic here," Seldanna said.

"Correct. After the first prisoner's escape attempt ended in a bloodbath, the sitting councilors expanded the protective spells to cover the entire building since the first safety net only covered the cellblock specifically," Conall answered, his voice level enough that he could have announced that the dining hall started serving the next meal. "This way seems less ideal, but trust me, this is a much safer alternative for all involved."

"They're all bound with spells. How do we undo those?"

"We don't have to worry about that. The spells' anchors should stay intact long enough after entering the building to get them into their cell before the spells fizzle. I don't know the full workings of the whole system, but something in the net of spells that cover this building breaks down other spells overtime once they cross that threshold. I find it fascinating that someone thought of such a feature, but I have never studied any of that to know how or why it works. Supposedly before the war when the headmasters changed hands, a more formal process existed for understanding all of this, but some of that fell to the wayside as other priorities took place."

Seldanna rubbed what felt like weeks of sleeplessness from her eyes. "What is your plan here, Conall?"

"I intend to stop the war," he replied calmly.

"Your predilection for vague answers is one that I hoped would stop when you stepped into the role of Archmage," Seldanna said and paused for a second to see how he would respond to her snark. "How are you going to end the war?"

"Right now, I'm not quite sure, but don't worry though, I will find a solution."

"If you're as determined as you are ambiguous, then we have nothing to worry about. I'll go upstairs and bring Celeste down. Do I need any keys for any of the rooms while you are gathering help to deal with Troy?"

"No, you don't need a key to set the locks on the cells, and that should be the only interaction you should have to deal with. Everything else should be open."

"How long do you think it will take for you to recruit some help?" Seldanna asked as they started ascending the stairs together. The walk up the stairs was easier than the walk down, but she expected that since she wasn't currently carrying another person on her shoulders.

"I shouldn't be long," Conall said, opening the door to the outside for Seldanna. "Do you need anything before I leave?"

"I should be fine."

"I will return shortly," Conall said as he opened a portal. A moment later he stepped through the shimmering doorway in the air and disappeared back into the gloom that clung to Arngan Field. Seldanna found herself wondering how long it would take for the rest of the Children of Chaos to notice someone kidnapped their leaders. How would they retaliate?

She shook the thought from her mind as that was entirely out of her control from here. There were enough others on the war council to skillfully execute any necessary defensive measures. With her thoughts broken from the battlefield, she briefly thought about Wollarr and the other survivors from the strike team. She breathed a prayer for Almar and Eldrin, hoping they would pull through their injuries. She didn't know the extent of what happened to Eldrin, but knew blood covered much of his face, especially around his mouth and nose. Both he and Almar fell unconscious before Wollarr could carry them through the portal on his way to take them to the healers.

Seldanna briefly touched her right cheek with now-faded scars she earned during the previous war and reminded herself of the healers' skills. Several in their camp would tend to Eldrin and Almar.

A bird's series of lilting chirps nearby brought Seldanna's attention back to the forest around her, and she looked around briefly to find the bird to no avail. Shrugging her shoulders, Seldanna returned to her current task and climbed into the back of the wagon to retrieve Celeste. She grabbed the ashen-haired Mage and lifted her enough to place her near the edge of the cart before climbing back down the three flat rungs. With the edge of the wagon's bed coming up to her stomach, Seldanna found it easy to get Celeste onto her shoulders on her own. Under burden again, she made her way inside and back down the stairs toward the cellblock as quickly as she could without falling or dropping the Mage she carried. Celeste felt lighter than Aska and that alone made the task of carrying Lillis's younger sister down the stairs easier. The process still involved Seldanna's legs trembling as she slowly descended the stairs, but it felt easier at least.

Once at the bottom of the stairs, Seldanna opened the door to her right and made a beeline for the cell next to Aska. She opened the iron door and set Celeste down inside before stepping back out into the walkway, closing the door, and setting the lock the same as she saw Conall do earlier. Seldanna turned to her left and as she was about to leave the cellblock, felt eyes on her. She turned and jumped. Lillis stood at the door to her cell, her eyes locked on Seldanna, and her long, slender fingers wrapped around the iron bars that formed the door to her cage. Her face showed no expression other than her eyes which still burned with the same rage Seldanna saw before in the

Children's command tent during the strike and again when Lillis was in the back of the wagon. Even before the Betrayal, Seldanna never felt comfortable under Lillis's gaze. Something about her back then felt unnatural, and, after the Children broke away from the College and the war started, Seldanna assumed this alignment was a major part of that sensation. Now, locked in the cell as she was, trapped behind those iron bars, and contained within this dungeon with everyone cut off from their Magic, Seldanna still wanted to shy away from Lillis. The intense heat in those pale blue eyes made her knees want to buckle.

"You're uncomfortable," Lillis said, her voice low and rasping like days passed since she last spoke to anyone.

"What gave that away?"

"You never did talk with me more than absolutely required, Seldanna."

"You're an imposing person, Lillis. I can see why you above anyone led the charge to destroy this world and all we know."

Lillis laughed, the sound so genuine and gleeful but somehow also hollow. "You know so little of what we wish. Is this the rumor that spreads through your ranks? That we desire to destroy this world? Such a goal would be easy and would require little effort at all."

Beads of sweat formed on Seldanna's forehead, but she refused to wipe them away for fear that it might give Lillis a sense of victory or superiority in this moment. "If your desire is not to destroy the world, why go through all the trouble of starting this war? So many have died because of your choices."

"The questions you ask make me wonder if you wish to join us. What would you do after gaining this information you desire?" Lillis asked, but Seldanna remained quiet. "You don't want to know our plan. No, that's too plain. You wish to understand why we left, what motivates us."

"She wants to purify us, sister," Celeste said from behind Seldanna.

"She has hope that we can return to her path," Aska said.

Seldanna slowly turned around and saw the other two Mages now standing at their cell doors, pressing themselves against the iron bars. Aska bared her teeth and bit the air in front of her. All three Children cackled when Seldanna jolted at that display. Seldanna felt her heart thumping in her chest and took a step backwards but bumped into the wall at the back of the cellblock before bolting toward the door at the other end. As she ran, Lillis called out through the bars that contained her.

"You can only delay the inevitable, Seldanna. Kalathan *will* enter this world. He longs to devour the mortal realms. Nothing can stop what we set in motion. Conall may strike us down if he so wishes, but others will fill the void we leave behind." Seldanna pushed the door open and heard all three of their voices join as if a trance ensnared each of them.

"We are legion, Seldanna," they said a moment before the door closed.

Once the door closed and Seldanna knew Lillis and the others in the cells couldn't see her, she gave in to the tears that welled inside her. Kalathan! Seldanna, like others among the Praetors, heard rumors about what the Children of Chaos sought. Hearing Lillis spew the Light Eater's name without any sense of hesitation drove a spike of fear deep within Seldanna's soul. Few said his name at any volume higher than the quietest whisper and even then, not without first looking around to see who would hear whose lips the name passed.

Seldanna let herself cry, doubled over with her hands against her knees, before composing herself and wiping the sweat and tears from her face. She felt her nose dripping and wiped her face on her sleeve. Taking a deep breath, she set off up the stairs to retrieve Serena from the wagon. She dreaded this more than anything else. She would prefer attempting to carry Troy to his cell on her own than carry such a close friend into this dungeon. Fury roiled deep within Seldanna's soul as she climbed into the wagon and moved Serena to the edge to retrieve her easier.

She stepped over Troy's bound legs and paused briefly to gaze at Serena while the heat continued smoldering inside her. Seeing the slender, graceful Mage's chestnut hair that somehow remained untouched by age and the smoothness of her face that retained the innocence from her youth, Seldanna clenched her fists. How could she choose to hurt Virion so thoroughly? All these years later and Seldanna still only saw the pain Virion faced when she learned Serena left her and joined the Children. She remembered the times the three of them ate dinner together and talked of what they wanted to do later in life. They spent untold hours chatting over empty glasses stained by the wine they drank, but Serena threw all of that away for *this*.

Seldanna climbed down the small ladder at the back of the wagon and took a deep breath through clenched teeth before shuffling Serena across her shoulders. Despite lecturing Neldor about the Children still being people, Seldanna wished she could allow herself to be less careful while carrying Serena. Perhaps that would relieve some of the fury she felt toward the friend she felt closest to before the war. She wished more than anything that Serena could experience the pain she caused Virion but knew revenge and justice were different. Revenge suited no one and doling out justice wasn't a task for Seldanna. Still carrying Serena across her shoulders, Seldanna took a deep breath and held it for five seconds to calm herself, then started walking toward the stairs.

Seldanna stepped through the door and felt her connection to her Magic cut off, something that, as Conall warned, felt unusual no matter how many times she experienced the sensation. It felt less like snuffing out a candle and more like everything close to the candle ceasing to exist after extinguishing the flame. One second, she saw the warmth and light in her mind that Magic gave her and in the next instant that cut straight to darkness. She shook off the feeling of being powerless and continued walking down the smooth stairs into the dungeon. With each step she passed stones in the walls with moss and moisture clinging to their surface. Few dry areas existed in this building, and she wondered about the safety of this structure. Still, it only needed to house their captives long enough for them to later see justice.

When she stepped off the bottom step, Seldanna again turned to her right so she could open the wooden door that stood between her and the cells. Unrelenting dread ballooned inside her as she reached for the iron handle on the door, but she swallowed the lump that formed in her throat and ignored her fluttering stomach. She pulled the door open and stepped fully into the cellblock. To avoid facing Lillis and the others again, Seldanna opened the first cell to her left inside the door, placed Virion's former wife inside, and set the cell's lock. She wasted no time waiting to see if any of the prisoners acknowledged her presence, nor did she look to see if any of them still stood against their doors before pushing open the wooden door again and leaving the cells behind her. Looking around the dungeon's main room, she considered sitting at the table while she waited for Conall to return, but decided instead to wait for him where she could feel her Magic. The chill from the spells severing her, even temporarily, made her skin crawl. She remembered how the College severed the Dark Mages who survived the first war and pondered if this was how they felt. Thoughts inundated her mind as the thought of living without her Magic overstayed its welcome. She walked up the stairs once more while the panic festered inside her and eventually settled on the stone stoop outside the iron door, basking in the sunlight for the first time since the Children cast their spells that changed the weather over Arngan Field. The warmth on her face and the return of her Magic after exiting the barrier spells helped drive away the terrible thoughts that brewed like a storm inside her.

Chapter Fourteen

Seldanna's eyes snapped open when she heard Conall and his recruited help straining as they worked to move Troy from the wagon toward the dungeon. She blinked quickly as her eyes again needed to adjust to the foreign sunlight streaming unhindered through the treetops. She couldn't remember falling asleep on the stone steps, nor did she know how much time passed between when she stepped outside the dungeon and now. The skin on the back of her neck burned and her muscles ached as she lifted her forehead off her wrists and straightened her back. How much time passed hardly mattered now, she told herself. She stood on the stoop and skittered out of the way as Conall, Wollarr, and Neldor carried Troy down the stairs, their grunts and groans telling of their struggle as they bore his massive weight. They stepped through the door and when Conall returned a long moment later, trails of sweat shimmered across his face from the exerted effort.

"I see you managed on your own with the other three. Hopefully it was uneventful?" he asked, wiping his brow with his sleeve.

"Something happened after I put Celeste to her cell."

"What do you mean by 'something happened' Seldanna?" Conall asked.

Seldanna thought the tips of his ears twitched but figured that easily could be the wind moving them. The breeze cutting through the trees felt nice despite its unexpected strength. She briefly recounted the events from earlier, ensuring that she mentioned everything she could remember Lillis saying. Even though she censored 'Kalathan' from her recounting, Conall looked no less concerned. Sweat once again trickled down the sides of his face. Neldor and Wollarr reached the top of the stairs the moment that Seldanna finished her retelling, adding to the stress she felt describing the encounter.

"We have to deal with these animals before they follow through with this plan, Conall," Neldor said. "Taking them before even the closest magistrate is a risk we cannot afford."

"We could bring one here," Wollarr suggested.

"That would eliminate almost all of our issues," Seldanna said.

Conall wiped his right hand down his face and sighed. "An easy solution doesn't exist."

Neldor's knuckles crackled as his fists clenched. "Not every decision you have to make will have an easy solution, Conall."

"We should take this to a vote among the war council. I don't want to make this decision without input from everyone. How we stop the war should be a mutual decision," Conall said.

"Stop being childish and make a decision," Neldor snarled, spittle flying from his lips.

"I didn't ask for this pressure, Neldor. What do you want from me?"

"I want you to act like you belong in your position."

"Watch your tone. I've abided your jealousy for too long," Conall snapped.

"As Archmage, these tough choices are yours to make," Neldor grumbled after taking a second to think through his response. "I am going back to our camp where I don't have to watch this gentle, spineless leadership falter like a galleon at sea without wind in her sails."

Without waiting for a rebuttal from Conall, Neldor opened a portal and walked down the stairs, jostling into Seldanna's shoulder as he stepped by her. Before disappearing through his portal, he stopped and turned around, his one eye locked on Conall with more intensity in his gaze than Seldanna ever saw there before. Conall stood at the top of the stairs, his arms crossed over his chest, stared back at Neldor, equal heat in his gaze. Seldanna had never seen such tension between them. Finally, Conall caved and spoke with a roll of his eyes.

"Speak your mind, Neldor. You know I prefer honesty from others over them holding their tongue for my benefit of my feelings."

"Do you want honesty? Your caution to watch my tone says otherwise."

"That comment was for your obvious insubordination. Speak your mind."

"Stop worrying about what others will think of the decision you make and just choose something. Stand by your choice in this. Every decision you make as the Archmage will come with hostility from any direction. Those who disagree with you, condemn you, or say how they would have made the decision differently are merely spectating. Anyone who isn't here but is telling you how to lead has no knowledge of the weight of command. There is no way they can understand the struggles we endure in this moment."

"You've never spoken so flowery before in your life. Say what you want me to hear or step through your portal," Conall said.

Neldor again clenched his hands tightly into fists and took a deep breath before speaking. "Make the correct choice here, Conall. By that, I don't mean the choice that lets you avoid the most judgement but the one that saves the world most effectively. If Lillis and her followers truly intend what they say, a judge won't stop them. Every moment they breathe is one that could spell disaster. Prison bars and sanitization cannot stop their plan from coming to fruition."

Conall lowered his head slightly but said nothing in return. The tension between them deflated quickly, and the veins in Conall's forehead and neck recessed. Seldanna couldn't remember seeing such indecision from him since shortly after he rose to his current position as the Archmage after his predecessor died. Hagen, while not killed in battle, succumbed to an aggressive sickness that came because of a wartime injury. His passing devastated the war council but seemed to hit Conall the hardest. It was the first instance of someone in that position not retiring or dying of age since the Betrayal. As a result of Hagen's death, Conall pulled the war council away from the battlefield to lead strategically but only after hours of back-and-forth discussion, much like happened now.

Conall pressed his thumb and finger against the bridge of his nose and sighed. "Neldor, I'm coming with you back to the camp. Seldanna, I will send Radelia and Virion here to keep you company. Do you mind staying here until I come back?"

"I'll be fine sitting here as long as you don't take too long."

"I don't anticipate this taking longer than an hour. The others should be here soon."

Seldanna touched Conall's shoulder gently. "I should be fine then. I'll stay out here. You did warn me about this, but not having my Magic is a sensation I don't enjoy."

"Whatever pleases you. Wollarr, can you please make sure the cart returns to the College stable. Thank the groundskeeper for letting us borrow it."

"Certainly," Wollarr said, walking down the steps and climbing onto the bench. He didn't wait for further instructions before grabbing the reins and setting off.

Neldor stepped through his portal with Conall following closely. The doorway stayed open for only a second after both Mages vanished before disappearing itself. Portals normally closed fast, but this one closed so quickly it reminded Seldanna of a grumpy child slamming a door shut after a parent denied them promised sweets. Alone again, Seldanna sat on the top step and rested her elbows against her knees and her chin nestled in her hands while she watched the wagon disappear into the forest. Wollarr turned right at the crossroads and soon dropped out of sight. Only her thoughts and the distant chattering of birds and squirrels accompanied her now.

"Allfather above I hope they're lying about their intentions," she whispered to herself.

Chapter Fifteen

No amount of time spent in this dungeon would let Seldanna enjoy not having access to her Magic. The absence of that light normally shining in her mind left her feeling vulnerable, cold, and naked. Sitting on this rickety chair with its peeling veneer and rough surface without a stitch of clothing would feel more comfortable, even with Virion and Radelia in the room, compared to not having Magic at her beck and call. For a brief second, she thought that having the whole war council here staring at her in such a state would be less uncomfortable, but her cheeks started warming at the thought. Ice shot up her spine at the thought of Neldor's one eye looking her over. Even though Conall warned her, and she admitted as much, the reality was worse than anything she expected from his mention of the barrier spells. She would prefer to sit outside, but the forest grew too chilly after the sun set and at least here there wasn't any wind.

She had no real way of knowing how much time had passed since Radelia and Virion arrived at the dungeon. Conall said he didn't anticipate taking long, but it felt like he said that at least two hours ago before he vanished through the portal with Neldor. What could he possibly be doing that would be more important than dealing with the Children? Seldanna's leg shook under the table, the only visible sign of her anxiety. Sitting at this table, waiting for Conall to return, she wondered how Virion and Radelia fared, but the latter's pacing spoke volumes even with her otherwise silence. In fairness, Radelia handled most waiting around poorly, much like a herding dog without any livestock to supervise. Falling into her normal pattern, Virion sat so still she may as well not be in the room at all, her thoughts taking her entirely elsewhere.

With Virion sitting statue-still at the table, Seldanna found herself only able to think about the small flame that danced on the candle's wick and the sound of Radelia pacing across the room. At least letting herself get distracted like this kept her from focusing on imagining what could possibly be in the room to her right that no one entered since they arrived. Radelia took five steps, stopped, turned, walked another five steps back to the other wall, and repeated that process. Radelia and Virion arrived at the dungeon earlier, not long after Conall and Neldor left through the portal outside. Radelia entered the dungeon immediately, but Virion sat on the steps with Seldanna while they admired the fading sunlight in the woods. Virion offered Radelia a spot where she could sit on the stoop, but she only received insistence that someone should stay inside to keep a close eye on the Children.

When Seldanna and Virion eventually came inside, Radelia was with the prisoners still. Virion took a seat at the table, and Seldanna sat with her to keep her company, which also gave her an excuse to avoid facing the Children again. Thinking about her earlier experience in the room with Lillis and the others, Seldanna still felt a wave of ice creep up her spine, bringing with it a shiver and the small bumps across her skin that made her hair stand tall. Radelia eventually left the cell room and sat in the empty chair at the table with the others briefly before standing and pacing the room. The sound of Radelia turning, that whisper of her boot against the floor followed by the heavy clomping, made Seldanna so uneasy. Her hands clenched into fists in her lap. Words formed on her lips, but before she could say anything that would result in an argument between her and the hot-tempered Mage, the door opened upstairs.

The hinges moaned as the door opened and the sound reminded Seldanna of a tale she heard repeatedly as a child of forgotten women who died unexpectedly, often in the wilderness. Unmarried and unfulfilled in life, their spirits latched themselves to the land and cried into eternity, their voices normally only heard in whispers carried by the wind. Her village elder often said their cries marked the deaths of others. Hearing the door close, Seldanna suspected Conall finally returned. Radelia stopped pacing, and Seldanna stared at the stairs that she could see from her seat at the table. The sound of unhurried footsteps making their way down the stairs spoke more about who was coming down the stairs than had Conall announced his return audibly. He reached the landing, and as he turned and walked down the second set of stairs, Seldanna fidgeted in her seat, her nerves building as he took his time coming into the lower level of this building where she had no Magic. Time seemed to crawl slower than a jar of spilled molasses.

Throughout the war, Conall wore simple, dark clothes. He wore nothing that showed him to be in any kind of leadership position for the Lambent Praetors, let alone being the Archmage. As he reached the bottom of the stairs and the light from the candle on the table revealed him, Seldanna saw he now wore his formal Mage's robes, dark grey fabric with black accents, the livery of the Elven king in Anselin. His previous station before the outbreak of the war had been as the chief advisor in the king's court. Why Conall chose to wear these robes when his white College robes or even Archmage robes were an option, she didn't know. She would have to find out the reason later.

"I apologize for the delay," he said, stepping through the doorway. "I hope my absence hasn't caused any problems."

"Nothing to report on our end," Radelia said.

"How are the prisoners?"

"Lillis is standing at her door trying to stare a hole through the far wall, but the others are sitting on the floor."

"What's your plan, Conall?" Seldanna asked.

He said nothing but looked at the door to his left across from the cells and the Children. "Come with me."

Virion was the only one of them not to move, her eyes still locked on the flame atop the candle as it consumed the white-yellow wax. Seldanna and Radelia followed Conall to the door and into a small room with a single table and a pair of chairs sitting opposite each other. The room, half the size of the connecting space, felt cramped with all three of them standing in it. Conall walked around the table and stood behind the chair facing the door. Radelia and Seldanna remained between him and the still-open door until he made a motion with his hands, and Radelia turned and closed the door behind them. Conall stared at the center of the table that stood between them. He took a deep breath before looking up and clearing his throat.

"The Children die here. Tonight," he said.

"Conall you can't be serious!" Seldanna said. "There are laws and expectations for the treatment they are supposed to receive as prisoners."

"Seldanna, I can't believe you're defending them right now," Radelia scoffed.

"Easy now, let's not get ourselves into a heated fight about morals and ethics," Conall countered. "This is what must happen. We can't take them before a magistrate."

"I can't see any way that we can simply ignore this," Seldanna said.

"Lillis revealing her plan to bring Kalathan into this world tells me that they are beyond salvation. Our war council are the only people who know that these five Dark Mages are in captivity, so their status as prisoners is questionable at best. If nothing else, we are the only ones who will know about what happens here tonight."

"How are we doing this, Conall?" Radelia asked.

"Well, I figured," he said, reaching into his robes and removing a sheathed knife, "we would deal with this ourselves."

"You're suggesting we murder them right here?" Seldanna asked.

"It's not like we have gallows where we can watch them hang," Radelia said. "Even if we did, we would have to get them out of the dungeon."

"I found no easy solution to deal with this situation, and this is the best I came up with. I'm open to suggestions that don't involve giving our enemy time before a magistrate to dole out a legal punishment for their crimes. The longer we keep these five alive, the more time they have to ensure their plan gets set in motion to bring about the end of our world," Conall said.

"I want no part of this," Seldanna said, raising her hands and turning to leave the room.

"This whole operation was your idea, Seldanna," Conall said as her hand touched the handle on the door.

"You're putting the weight of *this* on me?" she gasped as she turned from the door.

"That's not what I'm saying here—"

"*My* idea was to capture the Children from their camp so we could take them before a judge and get a legal end for their actions. I did *not* suggest that we take the road of vigilantes or that we cherry pick laws as we want."

"You made your suggestion to capture them after I said I wanted to end the war. How are you the only one here who is surprised by what I want to do here?"

"I'm a bit surprised but only that this is the option you're wanting to take," Radelia said. "I figured you wanted the Children to die to bring the end of the war but didn't think you would choose such a personal method for that."

"I don't know a better way to do this," Conall admitted.

"So, your plan is that you're going to bring all five of them in here and slaughter them like cattle?" Seldanna asked.

"Don't be ridiculous, Seldanna," Radelia said. "Cattle have a function after death."

"Again, I don't know a better way to end the fighting and bloodshed. We are dealing with a snake, and if I sever the head the body should stop." Conall said.

"And if it doesn't?" Seldanna said.

"Honestly, that's a risk that I don't want to take but am willing to accept. Power abhors a vacuum, and we're going to make a big one here tonight," Conall said. "If their followers haven't already noticed their absence, they will soon. Neldor is preparing for the worst."

"They aren't strangers, Conall, we know all five of them. You speak of them like they are objects to do with as you please."

"Exactly, Seldanna. None of them are strangers, yet they still betrayed us like we meant nothing to them. Have you forgotten what they did to Gilros? To the Council? I will never begin to understand why they made the choices they have or what led them down the road they are on, but that is not my place to understand or judge. What I know, here and now, is that if we let them live, more lives are in danger than I want to account for. They don't threaten only the College and our way of learning and teaching Magic. They are threatening the *world*, Seldanna."

She took a deep breath and turned back to face the door. "I want no part of this. You have made your choice, and I will never agree with it. By doing this yourself, you are no different than them. They killed for what they believe in, and you are doing the same. Their blood is on your hands, Conall."

"Better the blood of five guilty than thousands of innocents."

"Don't try and bring a sense of moral high ground into this now, Conall. That ship sailed long ago," Seldanna said before storming out of the room, not wanting to hear any further argument on the matter. She slammed the door behind her and stomped her way to the table. All the noise together must have broken Virion from her trance because she jumped and finally looked away from the candle. Seldanna leaned against the table and growled, her eyes shut so tight she saw stars dancing around the inside of her eyelids.

"What's going on?" Virion asked.

"Conall wants to—" Seldanna started when the door opening behind her cut her off.

Radelia and Conall walked across the room from behind Seldanna and entered the cellblock. As they passed the table, both shot heated glares at Seldanna, and she did her best to show no reaction to their looks. She hoped her face looked less annoyed than she felt. Radelia opened the door to the cellblock and Conall walked through first. The door closed behind them a moment later and Seldanna felt her body try to collapse under her. She slinked into a chair and exhaled every bit of breath from her lungs. A look equally confused and concerned washed over Virions face, something that rarely happened with her. She reached a hand across the table to Seldanna who pulled away from her and leaned backwards into her chair.

"What are they planning?" Virion asked.

"He's going to kill them," Seldanna said, her lip trembling as she spoke.

Virion's face once again showed her normal lack of emotions as she considered this news. "I assumed he would choose that since we started this whole endeavor to capture them."

"Are you ok with this, Virion?" Seldanna asked. "Serena is—"

"Not my wife anymore, Seldanna. What happens to her doesn't affect me."

"But don't—" Seldanna started when the door from the cells opened, cutting her off again. Radelia walked in front of a slender woman wearing a burlap hood over her head and rope that bound her hands to themselves and her waist as well. Radelia held the end of the rope like she held nothing more than the leash for a calf she guided to the slaughterhouse. Even without seeing the prisoner's face, Seldanna knew this was Serena. Her frame and size alone were unmistakable among the Children of Chaos. Why would they start with her, and with Virion sitting right here? This choice felt cruel for the sake of cruelty. There was no accident in this.

Radelia's face showed no less anger toward Seldanna than it had moments before. Conall sauntered behind Serena and closed the door to the cell behind him, using his body weight to ensure the latch set. He leaned against the door with his eyes locked on Seldanna as she watched Serena head to the other room. Seldanna's heart fluttered in her chest. Something needed to be done. There had to be something she could do to derail Conall from this path, but she knew from the sheer determination on his face that he would hear no more arguments from her about this. He clearly came to terms with his decision on this matter even before he came back. Seldanna had few gripes about Conall, but his stubbornness certainly topped the list.

Seldanna finally dropped her eyes from Conall's stare and watched the wet blurs that grew on the side of her eyes, her vision growing fuzzy. She refused to let any of these tears leave her eyes while he could see her. She refused to give him that amount of satisfaction. Keeping her eyes downcast, she watched him cross the room and heard the door behind her close before she blinked and felt warmth stream down her face. Her bottom lip quivered, and something ran from her nose down her upper lip. She wiped her sleeve across her face and looked to Virion for even just a crumb of comfort about the situation that she might have.

"Seldanna…" she whispered, her voice soft and near breaking.

"I'm so sorry that they chose her to go first. It's unfair that they would parade her in front of you like that," Seldanna said.

"I appreciate your concern, but it's unnecessary. She hasn't been my wife for over five years. I noticed a rift existed between us even before the Betrayal. In the two months leading up to that event, she seemed unlike herself. I assume now that that marked the events that solidified them in their choices."

"How can you say all of that so calmly, Virion?"

"I made my peace with this situation, tough as that may be for others to hear. Everyone assumes that I am fragile and delicate, a piece of fine pottery that must be always guarded. I couldn't be further from that reality."

"So, you're fine with Conall and Radelia taking Serena in that room to kill her?"

"I'm far from *fine*, Seldanna," she said. Her lower lip trembled slightly, but she sighed and locked eyes with Seldanna before speaking again. "Mages have fought our own kind too long. How many have died in these wars? Do you think we will ever have true peace again? How much has this war alone stagnated our ability to advance society? I don't know if what happens here tonight will bring about an end."

"Conall seems to think that—"

"There are many strong opinions on the council, Seldanna. This isn't an easy situation to navigate by any stretch of the imagination. Fishermen have avoided fewer obstacles in the shallowest rivers than we face here. Conall has made a choice he hopes will solve a bigger piece of the picture than any of us can see. You and I can't look at what's going on here in this dungeon and form an opinion of right or wrong based on this alone. The fighting rages in the trenches, the threat that the Children pose to the world still exists."

"This is wrong though."

"Everyone alive right now has paid such a significant price because of this war. How many more lives do we risk losing waiting for the politicians to navigate their way through the fog to a solution that may not work anyway? They could concoct a solution that ends up making the entire situation worse, too."

"We have laws for a reason, Virion."

"We do. But those laws were there before the Betrayal, and despite that truth, they still stopped none of what the Children did."

"If we sit here and let this happen, are *we* any different than the Children when they started this war?"

"Is that a better prize to seek than preserving life itself? What do you want from this effort, Seldanna?"

"I don't know, Virion. I am not fine with what Conall and Radelia are preparing to do in that room. I can't live with myself knowing I could have done something more to stop it. On the other hand, I am tired. No one has slept soundly in years."

"War has prices no one expects to pay," Virion said.

"How can I just act like I'm fine with this?" Seldanna asked after a moment of silence.

Virion again fell silent for a long moment before she looked at the door over Seldanna's right shoulder. "I may have a solution for you. It will change none of what is going on here—"

Punctuating her sentence perfectly, a shrill scream erupted from the other room. It lasted only a moment, but it felt like an echo filled the room for entire minutes after it stopped. The sound alone froze Virion where she sat. Seldanna didn't see Virion blink for such a long time that she grew concerned for her. Finally, a moment later, movement reclaimed her, and she set her hands flat on the table and stood. She motioned for Seldanna to follow her up the stairs and together they walked toward the stairs.

"I saw a healer after the Betrayal and that helped more than I expected. She cast a spell that she said works much like a colander. I don't fully understand how it works, but I know the spell well enough to help you live in peace despite Conall's plans."

"I don't know that I understand what you're talking about, Virion."

"I am probably explaining it poorly, but a lot of the memories about this moment can be stored somewhere in your mind. This spell doesn't purge anything from you, but instead will put some items in a box for you. It's the only solution I can think of that will keep what happens today from consuming you and leaving you a shell of your former self. We don't have to do this if you don't want, but it's an option to at least explore. This should also be reversible should that be something you want later."

"You said it helped you with the Betrayal?"

"It's what helped the best. Now there's also a chance this box may break someday, and all of this comes flooding back, and there's no way to know when or how or why that might happen. I asked the healer and she said sometimes these things just reach a point where the spell weakens beyond repair and will simply collapse," Virion said as they walked through the door and Magic returned to them both. "Is that something you're willing to risk?"

"I trust you, Virion. I know that this will consume me otherwise."

"Alright. Take a seat on the steps and I'll start. You might feel something when I get the spell planted…"

As Virion spoke the words, her voice seemed to slow down and Seldanna thought the world around her distorted until everything faded away altogether.

Chapter Sixteen

...In the Present...

Seldanna took the final sip of water from the cup on the shelf inside her lectern. With the empty glass returned to the shelf, she took a deep breath and scanned the room, looking at the faces of her students and wondering what they thought. Conall still leaned against the back wall with both hands behind his back but with his gaze now lowered toward the floor. His face showed little emotion, but she knew by his stance that he would have comments for her later, whether good or bad. Not once in the thirty years that have passed since the end of the war had she spoken of her specific experiences with anyone, let alone Conall. She assumed others on the team would have mentioned any of the events of the strike, but the concern on his face as she retold that part of her story suggested otherwise.

"Councilor, are the Children of Chaos still a threat?" Clara asked, breaking the silence.

Seldanna saw Conall's pointed ears twitch briefly at this question. He didn't lift his head, but any reaction from him was often enough to gauge his interest. She couldn't know what he thought of Clara's question, or if he would step in to answer, but she knew the council objected to open discussions about the Children to discourage unwarranted curiosity about the Dark Mages. Seldanna didn't agree with the idea of locking knowledge away, but she also understood not freely broadcasting information about Dark Mage cults. They made exceptions for classroom settings and lectures where they considered such a topic as normal or expected, but even so, broaching the subject still set the council on edge.

"You pose a difficult question, Clara," Seldanna said. "Before the Betrayal, we thought of Dark Mages as little more than a bad memory. The Assembly of Mages, as far as anyone could tell, died out after the end of the first war and the Treaty of Anselin. Whether or not there are still members of any cult of Dark Mages is impossible to say with any certainty."

"How can we live with such uncertainty? If they truly want to destroy our world, why would we not do everything in our power to stop them?" Adrian asked.

"The council spends much of our time trying to find an answer to that question," Conall said. "Unfortunately, it's not an easy task nor is it an easy question to face."

"It feels like it should be simpler though," Adrian replied. "If someone wants to destroy the world or is part of a cult, we should deal with them appropriately."

"In an ideal world, that mindset works, Adrian. The world is a complex place, and there are too many other parts to consider than a black and white policy could handle," Seldanna said. "This is a subject that often brings heated debate. It's often too easy to objectify someone who happens to be a Dark Mage. Doing so makes it hard to remember that they are still people. Not every Child of Chaos was as committed to destruction as their leaders were during the wars."

"Has the College allowed anyone to return here after joining these cults?" Clara asked.

"No," Conall said, his tone shifting to one of growing annoyance.

"Isn't that a harsh decision to make?" Clara asked, her voice indignant.

"It's not a risk we can or should be willing to take. They made their decision and should accept what comes with that," Conall answered.

"What about those pulled into that decision against their will? Shouldn't they receive grace and understanding, especially if they didn't all commit the same atrocities as others who chose to join the Children?"

"Again, Clara, this isn't a decision that is easy to make or one we reach lightly. If we could come up with a way to determine intentions or capabilities, we could possibly allow some to come back. Until then, we cannot back down on this choice," Seldanna replied.

"It feels like there are mixed signals coming from different members of the council. Headmaster, you are firm and decisive about this, but Councilor Seldanna is wanting us to accept the complexities of life and the world around us. I understand this decision is complex, but it also feels like one side outshines the other. How can we continue to fight for what we believe in when others simply drown us out?" Clara asked, looking back and forth between Conall and Seldanna.

"We learn to compromise, Clara. There are times when opinions get in the way of what is best for everyone. Of course, I would personally prefer that we rehabilitate those who feel remorse for their choices, but that's not a decision we can wait for. Life rarely contains wins for everyone involved. Enough of you here should attain the title of Master soon, and this is a lesson you need to understand sooner than later," Seldanna said as a bell rang outside announcing the coming end of the class period. "This lecture period deviated from the norm but breaking away from our expectations can benefit our learning. Be prepared for continued discussion tomorrow morning."

Chapter Seventeen

Conall stayed at the back of the classroom, leaning against the back wall with his hands tucked in his lower back between his body and the wall while the students all filed out of the classroom. Except when Neia, Ailas, and Adrian approached, Conall kept his eyes toward the back of the classroom. He locked eyes with the three troublesome students he asked to see after class, his eyes narrowing slightly as they approached the door at the back of the room. Seldanna saw most students turn right after leaving her classroom. Those three turned left before making their way to the headmaster's office. Clara, the only student who remained in her seat, stood when the classroom was empty and approached

Seldanna at her lectern. Her face showed layers of both concern and curiosity woven into a tapestry.

"Councilor, I wanted to ask some questions if you have the time," she said, her eyes somehow bigger than normal.

"What questions do you have?" Seldanna asked.

"Don't make yourself late for your next class, Clara," Conall said as he reached the bottom of the steps.

"Apologies, Headmaster," she said. Rosy spots formed on her cheeks as she backed away and scurried out of the classroom.

Seldanna kept her eyes on the slanted surface of her lectern and prepared herself for whatever feedback Conall had for her. The door at the back of the classroom closed behind Clara and the headmaster stepped to his left to stand in front of the lectern. Conall, slightly shorter than Seldanna, grabbed the end of the lectern facing him and leaned forward, waiting for her to look at him. She stared at the slanted surface of her lectern before she finally glanced at Conall. In this moment she noticed the faintest creases around his eyes and the grey smattered throughout his hair. Despite those signs of time's touch, there still seemed to be subtle hints of the boyishness she admired. In this moment, however, his eyes seemed stern and his face serious.

"Say what you wish, Conall," she said, not sure where she expected him to even begin.

"The war…" he started but trailed off then started over. "I've never heard any of what happened during the strike in their camp. I don't think I've ever fully known what happened there that night. I'm sorry you faced that. Had I known…"

"It's fine, Conall. There was a cost to ending the war. Every single one of us paid our share of that price. I went through that portal knowing there was a chance I wouldn't return."

"That hardly seems to justify what you experienced. I also didn't know what Virion did for you. She's never mentioned it, and I assumed your quietude was a personal choice you made more than a result of anything else."

"I think perhaps it could be a touch of both," Seldanna said, her voice raspy.

"When did these memories come back?"

"This morning. I had a nightmare that I was back in the dungeon waiting for you to arrive. I've had repeated visions as well since then, many of which have overlapped with reality. Clara came into the classroom on the tail end of the most intense one."

"Let me know if you need to take any time away from the classroom to process all of this. I don't want to lose you to the emotions we faced there that night."

"I appreciate that, Conall. I will tell you if anything gets to be too much," she said. "Can I ask you something?"

"Of course."

"Are you fine with the choice you made. Killing them, I mean."

Conall took a deep breath and looked away briefly before bringing his eyes back to Seldanna's. "Had we not intervened, I don't know how much longer the war would have raged on. We had already lost so many up to that point."

"You're skirting the question, Conall."

"I know," he said. "So often, I find it hard not to question if I made the right choice. There may have been other options, but none that I considered seemed like the right ones at that moment. It's easy to look back, knowing what's happened since then, and make better choices, but considering past possibilities with no way to change them does no one any good."

"If you can sleep at night, I suppose that's what matters most."

"The solution that benefits society often overshadows what aligns with an individual's wants or needs. I tried my best to consider the world's needs as I led the Praetors and since then as the headmaster here."

"I understand, Conall. These memories and emotions coming up now are still so raw to deal with. I will need time to grieve or mourn or whatever reaction is necessary."

"The Mages you captured that night were not the friends we knew before the Betrayal, Seldanna. Keep that in mind." Seldanna nodded but said nothing. "I should get to my office and address the students waiting for me. You have another lecture after lunch, yes?"

"I do."

"Let me know if you need a substitute for that. Process these memories as you need to," Conall said, placing a hand on hers and squeezing gently. "You're not alone in this."

"Thank you," she whispered. That was the most she could muster with her voice.

Conall stood there in silence, Seldanna's hand wrapped in his. He slowly removed his hand and nodded briefly before making his way toward the door. Seldanna remained at her lectern, staring at the wood grain pattern. Boulders replaced her feet, and sand filled her throat as thoughts whirled through her mind, wanting to form themselves into words that her body refused to utter. A single tear ran down her right cheek, falling onto the back of her hand as it sat on her lectern. Finally standing at the door, Conall paused for a moment and looked back at her. Despite only seeing him in her peripheral vision, she could sense remorse on his face. It radiated from him like the light from a lantern placed in a room. He said nothing and opened the door then walked out. Silence fell over Seldanna's now-empty classroom with the brief sound of a student running through the hallway the only noise to break the silence.

While Seldanna stood at her lectern, her body still refusing to move, the door to her classroom opened again. Her visitor surprised her, but seeing Virion step through the doorway made her smile all the same. Tight ringlets of steely hair framed her face, their shape maintaining her childlike appearance despite most of her black hair long ago fading to grey. She made her way down the stairs at a steady, indolent pace despite the faintest hint of a limp showing with her right leg. Not one to make a fuss about anything, she never complained about her hip without someone pressing her for details. She maintained her speed as she reached the bottom step and walked toward Seldanna. Reaching the small dais, she stepped up, approached the lectern, and placed a hand gently on Seldanna's shoulder. The warmth of Virion's hand transferred through Seldanna's robes in that same moment.

"Conall mentioned that the block on your memories broke," she said. "He also mentioned you may be having some difficulty with this."

Seldanna felt her hands release themselves from the lectern and she slowly turned to face Virion. "It's difficult having to process everything thirty years after everything happened."

"Some would call such a reality a blessing, but I think that negates your struggles, even if unintentionally so. When is your next lecture period?"

"Not until later this afternoon."

Virion hummed softly as she thought. "Why don't we get lunch? A walk and a change of scenery may help. What do you say?"

"Part of me wants to seclude myself, but I know that wallowing in this moment won't help anything."

"I won't force you to socialize more than you want. Come, let's see what food Helena and her staff prepared today," Virion said, stepping down from the platform and making her way toward the stairs. She moved without waiting to see if Seldanna joined her.

Seldanna stood at the lectern a moment longer before following Virion. She trotted to catch up and then matched her speed as they climbed the stairs. Each step was long enough that Seldanna needed to take one step forward before moving up to the next level. Soon she was at the door which Virion left open when she arrived earlier. Together they walked toward the dining hall. Except for three students heading the same direction ahead of them, they were alone. Still, they walked in silence. Like before the war, Virion largely kept to herself, if more ready to socialize now. Seldanna knew others privately judged her seclusion, but Virion never seemed bothered by that.

"I miss her," Virion whispered as they neared the dining hall.

Seldanna knew who Virion meant even without specific mention of Serena. "I don't blame you for that."

"My heart still aches when I think about her."

"You're allowed to feel that way, Virion."

"You are the only one who I think would see it that way after the war."

"The Betrayal made the Children our enemy. It didn't stop them being people. It seems difficult for too many to separate those two realities."

"Why do I still miss someone who did that to us?"

"You always loved her, Virion."

"Sometimes, I think I should change that."

"They say time heals all wounds," Seldanna scoffed. "That feels like it's more of a comfort for those providing the consolation than the ones receiving it."

"Time has done little except allow me to think of her less often. I suppose that could be a blessing on its own. Do you think that's what they mean by time healing wounds?"

"We can speak of something else, if you would prefer," Seldanna suggested as they entered the dining hall. She stepped to the right toward the kitchen where Helena and her staff worked tirelessly to keep dishes of food topped up.

"I appreciate your concern for me, Sel. There are such few people since the Betrayal who have continued to look after me. I think the others only did so during the war out of obligation."

"It pains me that you expect others to abandon you simply because your life endured sudden difficulties. That's not fair to you by any means," Seldanna said.

"I begrudge no one for their choices. Serena abandoning me doesn't require that others take on the burden of considering my emotional well-being. Everyone has their own lives to look after," Virion replied as she added some food to her plate and continued down the line.

"I know you don't intend that to sound so cynical and instead mean it to be blasé."

"Does the emotion I attach to the thought change the reality of the situation?"

Seldanna thought about that while she put more food on her plate. With her unblocked memories, Seldanna found herself in a similar situation as Virion. Former Praetors assumed she accepted reality or had no qualms with the situation simply because of her outward appearance. Did they care that little? The roar of students chatting at their tables throughout the dining hall made it difficult to think. Still, Virion's question was simple enough and shouldn't need a response.

"Let's go eat," Virion suggested, moving away from the food line toward the councilors' eating area. Seldanna followed, looking forward to sitting with her friend without any expectation to speak for the sake of filling silence. They reached Seldanna's typical table and sat across from each other and started eating their meals. This arrangement made Seldanna think of her breakfast with Elisen earlier and how this was so much different while sharing similarities. Save the sound of utensils against dishes, only silence accompanied them. Seldanna got through three bites of her lunch before Radelia ran toward their table.

"Thank the Allfather I found you both." Radelia said, her voice beyond flustered.

"What's going on?" Virion asked, immediately put on edge.

"Conall called a surprise council meeting. He needs us in the council chambers now."

Chapter Eighteen

Council meetings happened regularly, twice weekly unless someone was ill, busy, or otherwise indisposed. Due to the frequency of these meetings, they rarely lasted long. Seldanna could think of only one that lasted longer than half an hour in the past year. For Conall to call an off-schedule meeting seemed odd in and of itself, but for it to happen on the same day as the resurgence of her memories left Seldanna wondering about the correlation of those events. Surely the headmaster would have other motivations, especially with their next regular meeting scheduled for the following afternoon. Seldanna tore her eyes from Radelia and looked to her plate of half-eaten food and sighed before looking at Virion who somehow looked lost.

"I know you said 'now' but how urgent is this meeting?" Seldanna asked, looking back at Radelia, who still wore her hair in a tight braid all these years later.

"We don't have much time. I'll open a portal to get us to the council chambers."

"Can we first—"

"Leave your dishes, Seldanna. I'm sure Helena will understand," Radelia said, starting a spell. "She may even withhold the lashings she would normally order for anyone who leaves any dirty dishes at a table."

Seldanna wished the humor in Radelia's voice were less necessary. The head of the kitchen only ordered one student lashed during her tenure and, to this day, rescinding that punishment remained the only instance where Conall stepped on Helena's authority over the dining hall. Seldanna wondered what deal Conall struck for her appeasement, but such a subject was one she didn't need to discuss. Still, after one student receives a punishment of lashing for something as trivial as not taking dishes to the scullery, such an offense rarely happens again. Helena ruled her domain with an iron fist but doing so yielded undeniable results.

Radelia finished the portal spell and stepped through, not waiting for Virion or Seldanna to stand from the table, let alone acknowledge that they still sat at the table. Seldanna sighed and shook her head before standing from the table and walking toward the open portal. She looked over her shoulder to see if Virion was coming and to her surprise, Virion shadowed not far behind. They stepped through the portal within a second of each other and, once both stood fully in the council chambers, Radelia released the spell. Seldanna heard the faintest sound, like someone clapping their hands on the other side of a distant, closed door as the portal shut. She normally didn't hear that as she either didn't pay enough attention or the sound where her portals took her were too loud and drowned out the noise.

Despite maintaining her position on the council for more than two decades, entering these chambers usually left her feeling restrained awe, the same as when she first visited the College years ago. While no features of the council chambers were overly special or intricate, everything together made for an impressive room. Located perfectly in the center of the College's central tower, this was a circular room with white, fluted pillars all around the room, partially contained within the walls so only a half circle of each as they encompassed the room. On one side of the room stood a double door, the normal entrance to the chambers. Opposite the doors rose a dais holding seven chairs, with the central chair sitting on its own dais higher than the rest. Conall or whomever filled the position of headmaster sat in the middle chair while the councilors, the heads of their respective disciplines within the College occupied the chairs to either side. Behind the center chair, unnoticeable through the perfectly blended, patterned wallpaper, was a door leading to a private study the councilors used when they held open forums and needed a recess. When holding ceremonies, they also used that room for staging and preparations.

Plush, royal blue carpet lined the floor with a golden compass rose emblazoned in the carpet. Not actually aligned with proper directions, the north marker pointed toward the council's dais as a symbol that they served as a steady bearing. Whether they wished for only the College or the world to look to them for direction, Seldanna couldn't say. This room remained largely unchanged as long as she could remember. The walls carried the same color scheme as the floor except with smaller compass roses, roughly palm-sized, arranged in a visually pleasing pattern. The ornate plaster ceiling, white with gold accents, completed the look. Sconces around the room and a central hanging fixture cast light throughout the room. Long ago, candles illuminated the chambers but today, they relied on spells which provided brighter, more consistent light through the room.

"Does anyone know why Conall called this meeting?" Neldor grumbled.

"We will find out soon enough," Wollarr said.

"Just like him to call us here and then make us wait," the one-eyed Mage groaned.

The door behind Conall's chair opened as Neldor complained and closed with a whisper. Seldanna looked over Neldor's shoulder and saw Conall and a stranger standing on the dais. Conall leaned against his chair and the stranger, a man of indiscernible age wearing dark blue, hooded robes bearing a white wading bird centered on his chest, stood slightly behind him. Seldanna felt her right eyebrow raise as she wondered about the identity of this visitor.

Conall wasted no time waiting for Neldor to elaborate before speaking. "At least you have the stones to say that when I can hear it."

"I say nothing behind your back that I won't say to your face."

Conall stepped down from the dais and strode toward the clustered councilors in the center of the room. "I'll take that as reassuring."

"What's the meaning for this meeting, Conall?" Radelia asked. "Who is this visitor? I thought we agreed a long time ago that council meetings should remain closed affairs."

"Ordinarily, I would maintain that agreement and would have kept to that, but this situation is different," Conall said. "To explain, I would like to introduce Ilodon, a priest from the Order of Herons who arrived from Erith this morning."

"Greetings, councilors," he said, bowing slightly before continuing. "I apologize for the intrusion, but as Headmaster Conall said, this matter is of great import. Recently, my order has seen an increase in Madness. Monsters only seen in our world after the Assembly of Mages opened their rifts to other realms cause such a concern that Duchess Nalisa considers closing our fine city until we neutralize the threat they pose to her citizens."

"What monsters are you seeing near Erith? We haven't heard anything of this before now," Radelia said.

"Goblins mostly. They have taken to the peninsula across the bay from our city. They still wander near the roads when feeling brave. The larger concern are the werewolves."

"Is the Order of Herons asking for the College to exterminate goblins and werewolves?" Neldor asked, his tone filled with more annoyance than anything.

"I understand this appears trivial on the surface. We simply wish to bring this to your attention and express our concern. We need help with the werewolves as they have grown aggressive, and until recently we could handle them sufficiently," Ilodon replied. His face showed calm as he locked eyes with Neldor, something few managed after looking at his empty eye socket and the scars around it. "There are also rumors of a manticore brood in the area, but that seems unfounded."

Seldanna looked at the other councilors gathered in the room, surprised that none of them seemed concerned about the mention of these monsters. "You think a connection exists between the monster activity and Dark Magic use?"

Ilodon took a deep breath before answering. "I have not found a more logical connection than that. The Order receives many reports each week of attacks along the roads approaching Erith. Merchants pulled from their wagons or gutted where they sat, people reported missing but found dead and dismembered within a week, or families found slaughtered in their countryside homes where such things haven't happened before. Our Order exists as a bastion from Madness, but we can do little to protect our people from that without assistance. This is a difficult request since you have more significant resources available than us."

"Conall, what would you suggest we do about this?" Seldanna asked.

"I have a suggestion, unconventional as it may be," he said. "We need to form a new school, one dedicated to dealing with the Dark Mages."

"A new school?" Radelia asked.

"I hardly see a need for doing such a thing," Neldor grumbled.

"How would this new 'school' even operate?" Wollarr asked. "Would they have a councilor? After graduation, would students have the choice to pick that as their discipline?"

"An added councilor would break our quorum," Virion said.

"I was hoping for more support for this idea," Conall spat. "You all bring up great questions, and I want to answer them all. I only have a rough vision of how this works right now. We can work out the fine details later."

"What is your vision for this school's purpose?" Wollarr asked.

"I appreciate your collective enthusiasm but let me address the existing concerns before moving on to new ones," Conall said. "Virion, if we add a new councilor for this school, we can remove the headmaster from the voting pool to keep the quorum. As for the operation, I envisioned this school functioning as the council's sword, so to speak. By giving them a seat on the council, this school can operate with our authority across the continent. They would, under the direction of their councilor, snuff out Dark Mages and keep our world from approaching the brink of destruction that we approached with both the Betrayal and the war. How does this sound?"

"You say, 'snuff out' as if we aren't dealing with people," Seldanna mumbled.

"Not this again," Radelia groaned.

"Headmaster, I hate to interrupt, but if there is no further need for my presence, I shall return to Erith," Ilodon said, his voice still firm like earlier.

"Do what you must. Thank you for coming today. I will send correspondence after we have reached a decision on this," Conall said.

"Thank you for your time," Ilodon said before opening a portal between the cluster of councilors and the dais.

"Can we get back to discussing this school now?" Neldor asked.

"Certainly. Where were we?" Conall said.

"Seldanna had issues with Conall's word choice," Radelia sniped.

"That's nice, Radelia," Seldanna whispered.

"Let's keep things civil," Conall said. "I won't tolerate in-fighting."

"I just don't like that we so readily dehumanize our enemies simply because they walk a path which we neither allow nor understand," Seldanna said. "I don't want to fight about this, but they are still people. That's all I will say." Seldanna felt the warmth of a hand on her shoulder as she finished talking.

"Fine," Conall said. "That does bring me to the main item I wanted to discuss about this school and their operations. I want the councilor we select to run this school to have total control over their operations, just as with the other schools."

"What happens if the policy they have over their school causes problems?" Neldor asked.

"Give me an example of a problem you foresee."

"They uncover a Dark Mage and decide against killing them out of sympathy or some other soft-heartedness," Radelia said, sending a sidelong glance toward Seldanna.

"I already said I won't allow in-fighting. Let this serve as your last warning for the day, Radelia."

"It's a fair question to ask though, if worded a bit pointedly," Wollarr said. "If we leave the governance of this school entirely to the will of their councilor, we can find ourselves on either end of a pendulum where on one end they act too strictly and send their agents on witch hunts against anyone they dislike and hide this under the guise of saving the world. On the other they do nothing for fear of history judging them as too harsh."

"This school should operate separate from our influence," Virion said, removing her hand from Seldanna's shoulder.

"Explain," Conall said.

"We can't accomplish anything in a timely manner. If this school finds a previously unknown sect of Dark Mages but relies on us to figure out their course of action in dealing with that, we risk plunging the world into war again."

Conall scratched at the salt and pepper colored stubble covering his chin. "That was my fear and why I want them to have their own councilor. Perhaps we need further separation for this school. Thoughts on that?"

"Having this fall under a separate councilor is ideal. As a collective body we should be able to reprimand or replace the councilor as needed if issues arise," Neldor said.

"That's perhaps one of the more reasonable things you've said in your life," Conall said. "I forget that you have a tone other than crotchety."

"You shouldn't expect much more of that from me," Neldor muttered.

"I agree with Neldor that having that balance would prevent a rogue councilor from falling into Wollarr's pendulum situation. This also fits into our existing systems as well," Seldanna said. "That does still leave the question of staffing. Will students graduate into this school like the others?"

"I don't think that would be wise. I would prefer it if the existence of this school and those who run it remained a closely guarded secret. Ideally, I would want only the council, those selected as its staff, and the kings to know of the school's existence."

"Do we bend to their wills now?" Radelia asked.

"We still hold the power in our relationship with the kings. That said, I want them to think they are granting us this power. Mostly, I want them to recognize our authority with this new school should we have to send anyone to either Shemont or Anselin," Conall said.

"How much field work do you expect this new councilor to handle?" Venali asked, voicing her first question for this whole meeting. Radelia and Wollarr looked at her in surprise as if they forgot she stood among them.

"It's hard to say right now, but I would also leave that up to the councilor to decide as they wish. Do we have enough information to vote on this matter?" Conall asked.

"Let's get this over with," Neldor said. "I think this could have waited until our meeting tomorrow, Conall."

"I agree. Let's vote," Radelia said. "All in favor?"

"Aye," said Wollarr, Neldor, and Venali nearly in unison.

"Seldanna, Virion, either of you care to vote?" Conall asked.

"What's that?" Virion asked.

"We need to vote," Seldanna said. "In favor."

"In favor."

"There we have it," Conall said. "Now that we have created this new Dark Magic school, should we decide now who we should assign to the inaugural council seat?"

"It's no wonder we as a governing body can't do anything promptly. If we dropped this formality and voting shit, we could get things done a lot faster," Neldor said. "My suggestion is we slot one of us into that position and backfill that open council space later. All of us here saw the end of the war and should have no issues standing between the Dark Mages and the order they so readily want to destroy. Thoughts?"

"Fine. For now, we can set aside the formalities while we decide on a councilor. Would anyone else like to offer a suggestion?" Conall asked.

"I think we should give this position to Seldanna," Wollarr said. "She's level-headed and won't jump prematurely at the chance to shed blood when that decision comes up. Also, without her, the war would have ended differently."

"Seldanna is a good suggestion. I stand with Wollarr on this," Virion said.

"Same for me," Venali said. "Her or Radelia."

"I can't disagree with either choice," Neldor said.

Seldanna's heartbeat quickened hearing the suggestions go back and forth and tried to focus on finding a name to get the spotlight off herself. "What of Elisen?"

"She lacks the necessary experience for this," Radelia said without hesitation. "She was only just born at the time the war ended."

"That doesn't mean she can't want to stop the spread of Madness," Virion said.

"Is that the mission of this school? I thought they were finding and stopping Dark Mages. Conall?" Venali asked.

"One hand washes the other in this case," he said.

"If we put down Dark Mages as we find them, the Madness should spread slower," Neldor said. "I doubt the semantics matter this much."

"My objection stands regardless. Elisen is too inexperienced for a council seat. She's getting close but isn't there yet."

"Fine. So, then it's back to either you or me," Seldanna said looking at Radelia who currently gripped the end of her braid. Right now, seeing Radelia's braid under the light of the chandelier, Seldanna noticed that the coppery redness now showed large stripes of white from her head through her braid.

"I don't care if that is the choice, honestly. Conall, who do *you* want to fill this spot?" Radelia said, taking her gaze off Seldanna.

Conall scratched at his stubbly chin again while looking back and forth between Seldanna and Radelia. His eyes settled on Seldanna, and his hand dropped to his side before he spoke, his voice strong. "Seldanna."

"Is this what the council wants?" she asked.

"Enough of us mentioned your name. I don't want to force you to take this position if you are hesitant. I want someone dedicated and duty-bound for this position," Conall said. "Think it over if you need, but if there's nothing further, I think we can conclude here."

"When do you want to hear my decision?"

"By the end of the day is fine. Take your time with this."

"Thank you," Seldanna said before silence fell on the group.

"I'm heading to my office if we don't have anything else to discuss," Neldor said.

"I would like to finish my lunch," Virion said.

"We're adjourned. We can pick this up tomorrow during our normal meeting time. Thank you all for coming," Conall said as the councilors dispersed.

Virion opened a portal and motioned for Seldanna to follow her. Stepping through, they arrived back at their table in the dining hall. To their surprise, their half-eaten plates seemed untouched. As Seldanna sat down and Virion closed her portal, Helena approached carrying a plate in each hand. The softness of her face and relaxed gait suggested she was in a good mood. Perhaps "good" was too generous but time would soon tell.

"Councilors, Headmaster Conall told me he called an emergency meeting, and I set aside some food for you so it would still be warm when you returned. If either of you need anything else, let me know," she said, bowing her head slightly after she set the plates on the table and started to back away from their table.

Virion looked from the plate of food in front of her to Seldanna to Helena before she walked away and then back to Seldanna. "Have you ever had such an interaction with her before?"

"She's never hostile but also never that genuinely friendly," Seldanna said, scrunching her face before looking at the food on her plate. "I don't have much time to eat before I have to leave for my next lecture period."

"Ah, that's what I forgot to mention. Conall told me he found someone to cover your next class in case the memories coming back are too much for you. I was supposed to tell you earlier, but heartache and the council meeting took over."

"Well, that certainly changes things. How open is your schedule for the rest of the day?"

"The only thing I have planned is spending some time in the library to sort books, but that isn't until later this evening," Virion said, cutting through a soft piece of potato on her plate. "Do you know what you plan to do about this new appointment yet?"

"I really don't know what I will decide yet."

Virion swallowed the piece of potato before speaking. "What is your first thought? Those often seem to indicate our feelings on situations."

"I'm hesitant about it, if I can be honest."

"That's understandable. This is a new position that would require a lot of dedication—"

"My concern is less with the time commitment and more with the duties themselves."

"I don't follow."

"If anyone on the council defected, I couldn't bring myself to hunt them."

"Your concern is justified, Seldanna, but consider that—"

"I know that would be rare since everyone currently on the council fought with us against the Children, but it could happen, Virion, and it could happen easier than any of us would like to admit. They caught us by surprise once before; I doubt that will be the only instance of when that happens. A position like this comes with a heavy burden. One wrong identification of a Dark Mage, either positive or negative, and I would be personally responsible for lives lost."

"I do understand that. Seldanna, you are not the only one who dreads such a reality. I often wonder how life could have changed had any of us discovered the truth before the war started. Serena was my wife, and even with that I missed this in her. Perhaps if I had raised the question earlier, thousands of others might still be alive today."

"I can't live with that weight over my head, Virion."

"Then don't put it there. *You* are the one doing this to yourself. Keep yourself rooted in reality, rather than possibilities. I don't want to sway your decision one way or another, but I do want to make sure you aren't bullying yourself with possibilities."

Seldanna chewed a chunk of roasted chicken as she considered this nugget of wisdom. Worrying about possibilities was an unproductive way to go about making decisions, she admitted to herself. She never made decisions because of her anxiety before, why would she start down that path now? She never made hasty decisions either, but Conall did need her decision by the end of the day. For now, she could finish her lunch with Virion. She had a few hours until the day ended. Conall could wait for now.

Chapter Nineteen

Seldanna knew Conall's office well enough. As not only a councilor, but also a teacher here at the College, she spent her share of time in this room in various meetings with Conall, yet this was the first time where she stood outside his office and felt hesitation when she raised her hand to knock on the glass set within the top half of his office door. A decision made long ago, Conall's door bore only the word "headmaster" in bronze letters centered in the glass rather than his name. Even standing in front of his door, Seldanna could only see colored splotches through the glass, a result of the bumpy texture on the back of the glass. At the same time, Conall didn't see any more from inside than she could outside.

She knew her decision and made up her mind while talking with Virion during their lunch. Even with that, her arm refused to raise itself so she could knock on the glass and announce her presence. Two seconds later, her arm finally moved, rising toward the glass. She knocked and promptly heard Conall's reply from inside, somewhat muffled through the glass and wood door.

"Enter."

Seldanna opened the door and stepped in before closing the door behind her. Turning from the door, she briefly glanced around the room. A simple wood desk stood before her and to her left, in an alcove, she saw a sofa with a narrow table in front of it. Conall sat on the sofa, his white robes a stark contrast to the dark upholstery. His eyes remained locked on the book he held, rather than looking up to see who came to visit him. She doubted many students would willingly walk into this office, especially this late in the day, and he likely expected her after the council meeting earlier. She tried to see the title of the book, but the faded gold lettering against the equally subdued green binding made that harder than she expected. Most books with that binding style, a simple fabric adhered to the outer cover and words not inscribed on either cover but instead only on the spine, typically covered matters of law, and seeing Conall with such a book surprised her. Perhaps he wished to learn if any restrictions existed for the school he proposed at the meeting. She hoped he would have researched that before suggesting it at the meeting, but the presence of the priest from Erith could have delayed that. Unless he brought it up, she decided not to ask about the book.

To Conall's left, against the wall of the alcove beyond the edge of the sofa, a bookcase rose from floor to ceiling. Books sat on every shelf, some so fully that they stacked atop or in front of other books. Three shelves bowed under the weight of their tomes. Two others, also full, sat behind Conall's desk, a small, wooden floor cabinet between them; the door to the cabinet was closed, and Seldanna saw a keyhole in the door under the small, metal knob that long ago may have shown brightly but was now covered in a brown patina. A ceramic flowerpot with a miniature tree sat atop the cabinet. As with the singular bookcase to Conall's left, shelves on the two behind his neatly organized desk held more books than they had room for, and some bowed there as well. Two chairs sat between Seldanna and the desk, angled slightly toward each other so whoever sat in either chair would fully face Conall.

"What is your decision, Seldanna?" he asked, breaking her away from her look around the room. "I assume that's why you are here."

"Yes."

"That's wonder—"

"I'm sorry, I meant that yes I'm here about my decision."

"Oh. Well? Please don't leave me to guess your intentions here."

"I would never dream of doing such a thing," she said. "I accept the new position, though I have reservations about this decision."

"Excellent news. What has you worried?"

"My biggest worry is how to handle the Dark Mages after discovering them. In the dungeon all those years ago, you asked for my assistance in such a matter, and I couldn't bring myself to follow you down that path. I don't want to fall short—"

"Let me stop you there, Seldanna. I don't want you to worry about that. I don't expect you to personally kill anyone. That may come up at some point, but again, I don't expect that to be your main responsibility or even one that happens often enough that it should be a concern."

"You do expect it to happen though, otherwise you would have worded that differently."

"Come now, Seldanna, we both know that it's unlikely that you will have to fill the role of executioner while you serve in this role. Just be realistic and don't exclude it entirely."

"This likely would require an additional council decision, but what do you think about a tenure limit for the councilor's position?"

"How long were you thinking?"

"Four or five years should be sufficient."

Conall closed the book without any marker to remember his page and leaned back into the sofa. His brow furrowed, but a second later his eyes rose from the top of the table back to her. "That is reasonable. It would keep any single person from being too powerful or zealous while filling the position. I think the only thing the council needs to decide is the length of the term. I personally am leaning toward four years, but perhaps the others would prefer something different. Regardless, we can vote on that during our normal meeting tomorrow. Pending that, what is your decision?"

"I accept," she said. "I feel honored that you would consider me for this despite what happened in the dungeon all those years ago. I would have thought Radelia would be your choice for this kind of position."

"What makes you say that?"

"Come on, Conall, you can't be that dense. She's fierce, and we always thought of her as your brawn even if just coincidentally."

"It comforts me to hear that others think I need someone else to be my muscle."

"You know I didn't mean it like that," Seldanna said before seeing his wry smile and realizing the humor hidden in his words. "But you already knew that."

Conall lifted one of the cups from the tray on the table but paused before taking a drink. "Not everything is how it appears at the surface, Seldanna. I do agree that Radelia could be a good fit in the role, but I feel you are better suited for this. Her strengths lie elsewhere, and I think the council will find use for her elsewhere soon."

"I appreciate your vote of confidence. Time will tell if this is the correct choice, I suppose," she said, eyeing the empty cup on the tray.

"Care for some tea?" Conall said, seeing her eyeing the tray. "Beyond discussing your new position, I also wanted to make sure you are doing well with these memories."

Seldanna nodded and wasted no time preparing her cup after Conall offered. She filled her cup halfway and grabbed it to feel the ceramic as the tea warmed it. Weak steam tendrils wafted from the cup as she smelled the tea. She inhaled deeply trying to find all the scents from the tea. The tea gave off delicate jasmine scents with the crisp tinge of citrus following closely behind. This late in the season such a combination would be uncommon for almost anyone not living south of Shemont. She wondered what connections Conall had with the merchants who came near the College.

"There is a merchant I know through family who travels from Griffin's Perch to other areas in the continent. I bought this the last time I saw him, which isn't often enough. The tea isn't as fresh as I would prefer, but I can only ration it for so long before I question why I even bother buying it."

"It smells lovely regardless," she said before taking her first sip. "The taste is good too. Sorry, what were you asking?"

"How are you doing with your memories coming back? Virion explained the situation in shockingly sparse detail, even for her. I learned more about the process from your lecture than I did talking with her afterwards."

"It is funny how she can go into such lengthy detail over things that seem trivial to the rest of us but then glosses over things we really want to hear about," Seldanna said, taking another, longer drink of tea. "One of the many things that I find endearing about her."

"Agreed."

Seldanna returned her cup to the tray. "I don't want to keep you away from your book."

"No, please save me from this dreadful thing. There are few things I hate more than reading about laws."

"Are you taking up a new career?"

"I wish it were that simple. I'll tell you in a few days after I iron out all the details."

"How can you say something that is both vague and ominous at the same time?"

"I suppose that's one of my many, endearing talents."

"I'm serious, Conall."

"So am I, Seldanna. I am just looking into something for my own purposes but don't want to worry anyone before I have fully investigated this first. I should have an answer in a couple days and will share more then."

"Well, then I don't want to take more of your time than I have. Have a good night."

"You too, Seldanna. Congratulations on this new position. We'll formalize everything soon. Unlike other ceremonies, this one will be restrained given the new school's responsibility."

"Thanks, Conall," Seldanna said, opening the door and stepping into the hallway.

Chapter Twenty

...A few days later...

When Conall said before that the ceremony would be restrained, Seldanna figured that meant the ceremony would be so small it hardly made sense to even hold it. Based on the presence of the audience she sensed through the wall he clearly meant the ceremony would be more involved than that. She guessed that two dozen people stood throughout the council chambers. She assumed some of those would be the other councilors as they mingled with the attending guests. Sitting in the study behind the dais, Seldanna found herself feeling a strange mix of comfort and anxiety. The former she knew came from the soft, brushed suede covering the plush chair she sat in while waiting for the ceremony to start. As in Conall's office, this room contained many bookshelves, all of which were completely full of books. She had been in this room before, but she never spent enough time here to know the array of books well. She felt a great sense of envy seeing the rolling ladder attached to one wall's shelves. Perhaps someday she could have one of her own if she retired and settled down somewhere.

The door to her left opened a moment before Conall stepped into the study. His robes, the same pristine white that the other councilors wore, seemed to shine in the warm light coming from the small orb floating in the center of the room. He took a brief look around the room and pressed his hands together before speaking.

"I think we're about ready to start whenever you're ready," he said.

"You look more nervous than I feel," Seldanna said.

"About that," Conall started, a look of concern and guilt twisting his face. "I can't continue serving as the headmaster."

"You're retiring? This is beyond sudden."

"I'm *resigning,* not retiring."

"Please tell me you're joking."

"Far from that, Seldanna. I've only rarely been so serious before."

"Where is this coming from? You have been headmaster since the war ended and few have served the role as well as you."

Conall looked at the floor and sighed. "I can't pretend to be fine with the choices I made at the end of the war."

"You made the choices the Children forced you to make. You said yourself that you made the choice that bettered the world."

"The guilt from that choice eats at me daily."

"Why is this the first you've brought it up though?" Seldanna asked. "Is this because you heard my lecture the other day?"

"Not entirely." Conall brought his eyes to meet hers, an intense sorrow filling them.

"So that means I'm partially responsible. That's better," she said.

"Don't see it as being responsible."

"Conall, please don't do this for my sake. I may not agree with the choice to execute the Children, but I understand the necessity."

"The law disagrees with that," he said.

"Is that what you were researching?" Seldanna said, the realization hitting her seconds after the words left his lips. "Why would you search for something so damning?"

"I wanted to see if there was any exception to what I did so I could try to cast the guilt aside, but nothing in the law allows for my decision. You were right, Seldanna, they should have gotten a trial, even with the risk we evaluated in keeping them alive."

"The whole council stood behind you on this. You and Radelia aren't guilty—"

"You're right. She is wholly innocent. You and Virion weren't in that room to see, but she couldn't bring herself to kill them once the door closed. I gave her the knife, but she froze. I didn't expect that and took matters into my own hands, if only to save face with our prisoners."

"Wait, so this whole time, you—"

"Never told anyone else that Radelia's rigidity and roughness is largely exterior? Right. Between her desire to hide that her words were louder than her actions and the need to end the war, it was easier to never speak of that. She never asked for me to keep my tongue; her pride wouldn't allow that."

"Does she know you're telling me any of this?"

"You are the only one who knows. I also haven't mentioned my resignation to anyone else yet," he said, walking toward one of the bookshelves where a small, wooden box sat on a shelf. He opened the lid and retrieved a wax-sealed paper which he handed to Seldanna. "My official resignation and recommendation for the next headmaster is written here. Present this to the council after the ceremony finishes."

Seldanna held the letter in her hands, curious at how paper and a small glob of wax could feel heavier than a metal ingot. "Conall, don't do this."

"It's for my own sanity. You even said I need to sleep at night. I can't continue living this lie," he said, wiping a tear from his cheek with his sleeve. "Anyway, we should get out there before anyone starts to worry."

The door to the council chamber opened, and Radelia stuck her head in. "Conall? Are we doing this?"

"Of course. Just had someone's nerves to settle," he said, smiling wryly at Seldanna.

Radelia and Conall vanished through the door and, as it closed, Seldanna looked at the seal in the wax and felt the weight of everything Conall just told her piling on her shoulders. How could he just spring this on them and today of all days? As she looked at the seal, the council's compass rose serving as a steadfast reminder and guideline for others, she closed her eyes and sighed. If Conall thought he needed to make this decision, no one could sway him from this. She knew this news would ruffle feathers among the council and possibly the royals, not to mention the rest of the College, but she couldn't find it in herself to judge him for this choice. The others spent the previous thirty years dealing with the memories, emotions, and struggles that came with that night that ended the war. She gently traced her thumb over the compass sigil in the wax before tucking the letter into the pocket inside her robes. She stepped through the door and let it close behind her.

As she expected, roughly two dozen people stood in the council chambers. Virion, Neldor, Radelia, Wollarr, and Venali stood in front of chairs on the left side of the room as Seldanna faced them. Across the aisle between the chairs, she saw the royal families from both halves of the kingdom. King Elred and Queen Alea from Anselin and King Wilfred and his heir Prince Wolfram along with his betrothed, Princess Bera, filled the front row. Seeing King Wilfred now, his severely thinned, white hair, the slouch in his posture, and the weathered creases in his skin spoke volumes of his age. Hushed whispers speculated that Prince Wolfram would take the throne soon, but Seldanna held little stock in those rumors that started three years before when the king fell ill for over a year. Other members of the royal families filled the row behind the rulers, and behind the councilors stood the chief librarian and Helena who both served as heads within the College but weren't on the council for one reason or another.

Sometime before this ceremony, someone moved the chairs on the headmaster's dais to make room for both Conall and Seldanna as they stood on the platform for the administration of her oath. Since she had already sworn an oath of office when she originally assumed her place on the council, Seldanna knew what would come, which helped tame her nerves. Still, looking at the small group of people gathered for this brought a flutter to her stomach. Her secret knowledge of Conall's plan didn't help with that. She fought to not imagine how the other councilors would react hearing him announce his resignation. She wondered when he would break that news and hoped that he hadn't decided to announce it here and now.

"Good afternoon, everyone. I want to thank you all for coming today for what I believe will be a milestone day for not only the Sorcerer's College but also our ability to protect our world from Dark Mages and the threats they pose to life as we know it," Conall said. "I will administer the oath of office for councilor Seldanna as she assumes her new role as the first head of the newly created School for Dark Magic. Councilor, if you're ready?"

"Of course," she responded.

Conall grabbed a small, leather-bound book from a stand between him and the wall with the door to the study where Seldanna previously waited. "Please place your left hand on this book, which represents the charter for the College and the bylaws of our council, then raise your right hand." Seldanna did as instructed. "Repeat after me. I swear before the council and those present that I will serve honorably as the Head of the Dark Magic School. In pursuit of my duties, I will not practice any Dark Magic and will forsake anyone discovered as doing such, eradicating such as those from this realm. I will be the spear of the council and their instrument of protecting this world. Should I not uphold this oath, I request punishment to the fullest extent allowed by the council, to include death."

"...to include death," Seldanna repeated before modest applause erupted from those gathered to watch the ceremony.

The clapping only lasted a moment and as it slowed down, Conall gently grabbed Seldanna's upper arm, squeezed, and smiled before turning to face those gathered. "With that, I have an uncomfortable announcement. I am resigning my position effective immediately."

"Conall, what do you mean you're resigning?" Wollarr asked.

"Explain yourself, Conall!" Neldor nearly roared.

Before anyone could express further upset, Conall held up his hands and at least visually calmed the crowd. "I understand this news is unexpected, but I assure you all that I have my reasons, all of which I wrote in a letter which Seldanna now holds." Several eyes darted her way in the momentary pause before Conall continued. "With that said, I would like to recommend Radelia as my replacement. The council will need to confer on this, but I will leave that for you all to discuss later. For now, I take my leave. Your Majesties, thank you for attending today."

After a quick bow toward the gathered nobility, Conall stepped down from the dais and strode down the aisle in the middle of the room. He maintained his gait all the way to the double doors which he opened and stepped through almost without stopping. The hinges whispered as the wooden doors closed behind him. A moment later, the councilors were on their feet moving toward Seldanna, impatient to get their eyes on Conall's letter. Seldanna held off their voraciousness by holding up a hand and removed the letter from the pocket inside her robes. She showed them the unbroken wax seal on the letter and assured them she didn't know the contents of the letter itself.

"Right, that was unexpected," King Wilfred said before licking his bottom lip absently.

"Indeed," King Elred commented without looking at his human counterpart. "Come, my queen, we should make our way back to Anselin. Councilors, I appreciate the invitation to this ceremony. Councilors Seldanna and Radelia, we look forward to seeing how you handle your new positions. We will be in touch."

The human royal family also got up. Prince Wolfram walked down the aisle with his father, supporting the frail, elderly king as much as his stubbornness would allow. Princess Bera bade the council farewell before also walking toward the double doors herself. She kept her pace slower than the king and his heir to stay behind them. The lesser royals sitting in the second row also stood and walked out of the council chambers but said nothing. They were young enough that politics likely still bored them. Seldanna guessed they dreaded another time when someone made them wear courtly garb.

"Open the letter, Seldanna. We need to know why Conall left so suddenly," Radelia said.

Without objections, Seldanna broke the wax seal bearing the compass sigil and skimmed through the content of the letter before passing it to the other councilors. Radelia's free hand covered her mouth, and her eyes went wide as she read the letter which formally absolved her of any involvement in the Children's executions at the end of the war. Her hand trembled slightly as she passed the letter on to Virion who nodded as she read. Between her subdued reaction to the news Conall broke and her lack of facial expressions as she read, Seldanna guessed Virion knew of this decision before anyone else. Neldor received the letter next but couldn't contain his reactions before he finished reading.

"That's preposterous. None of us blame him for this decision except maybe Seldanna or Virion. The rest of us understand that war brings its own set of rules to follow."

"Drop it, Neldor," Radelia said. "We have bigger issues to address than your divisive opinions."

"Fine," Neldor growled. "Let's start with filling Conall's position."

"Seldanna will you be voting on this?" Wollarr asked. "I assume Radelia won't be as Conall named her as his suggested replacement."

"I will vote so we have a quorum," Seldanna said.

"All in favor?" Virion asked.

Epilogue

…Sometime in the future…

Conall never expected that he would stand before this building again. While the structure of the dungeon never approached being even remotely sound during his tenure as the Headmaster for the Sorcerer's College or prior as the Lambent Praetors' Archmage, time's passing only worsened it since the last time he stood before this iron door. Standing where he did, he still had access to his Magic but if he took another step forward, he would cross the boundary of the warding spells and would be without. He took a deep breath as he prepared for that feeling. He knew he wouldn't be here long, but he also knew that feeling cut off from Magic was not a sensation he wanted to drag out. Still, he needed to come here today.

He saw no point in delaying the inevitable and sighed before crossing the boundary and feeling that comforting bright spot in his mind fade in an instant.

He walked down the stairs and took no time to look around the room before walking to his left toward the same wood-and-iron door that concealed the choices he made decades before. He made those choices out of desperation and in the hope that it would bring peace. Largely, that was the outcome. The fighting continued for about two weeks after what happened here. He reached for the handle on the door, and dread filled him the instant his hand touched the cool, wrought iron. Beyond not expecting to return to the dungeon, Conall found himself about to open the one room he never wanted to face again. It was beyond time to face his past. He gripped the handle and pulled firmly, opening the door. The hinges moaned like wind racing across the moors north of Anselin and even further to the west along the distant coast. As the door opened, Conall's stomach tied itself into a monstrous knot he doubted would ever undo itself. Sitting on the center of the table where he left it was the knife he used that night. Stained and rusted, the neglected blade saw better days long before he left it here to slowly crumble into rust.

He stepped into the room, his legs at first hesitating to even move, and approached the table. Faded splatters of blood covered the table, a reminder of his repeated choices. His hand reached for the hilt of the knife, its blade littered with rusted pitting after decades of neglect. His fingers wrapped around the crumbling leather straps that still covered the wood pinned to the tang. He hated how familiar the knife felt even after sitting here for so long. He turned and strode out of the room, leaving the door open behind him, and slowly made his way back out of the dungeon. Memories haunted him with each step he took away from that room. He could almost see the looks on their faces as he slid the blade across their necks. Memories of Troy and Lillis bothered him the least as their eyes showed nothing but contempt for him. Thinking of Serena and Celeste, however, brought him the most grief. They looked nothing short of terrified in the moments leading to their deaths. Celeste likely defected because her sister led the Dark Mages, and she wanted even just a crumb of the same attention her sister garnered. A lifetime of sibling jealousy led to unnecessary anguish and untold deaths on both sides of the battlefield. Conall didn't know why Serena joined their ranks, but despite the regret he saw in her eyes, he still ended her life. He hoped to the Allfather that Virion could eventually find it within herself to forgive him for that. Whether he deserved such a kindness wasn't something he wouldn't consider right now, but he could still hope.

He reached the top of the stairs and walked back through the door back to the outside world. He closed the iron door behind him and used his key to set the lock. As if removing a tightly woven, wicker basket placed over a lantern, his Magic returned as he walked down the stairs. A lump formed in his throat as he opened a portal, but he stepped through knowing what he planned next needed to happen. His sudden presence in the king's study startled the Elf and caused him to dart to his feet from behind his desk.

"Conall, what is the meaning of this?" King Elred said a moment before the door to his study opened and two guards rushed in. Conall dropped the rusted knife onto the king's desk a second before the guards grabbed him firmly by the arms.

"I came here to give you everything you need to sentence me. This is the knife I used to kill five prisoners taken and held during a time of war. According to every law I can find within our kingdom, this is a crime punishable by death."

The king waved dismissively at his guards who released their grips from Conall's arms and backed away from him. "Conall, you already resigned from the College. These crimes you mention are so old that I cannot sentence you for them, not to mention they were committed during a war when additional lenience is granted. Others have committed worse atrocities in peace which resulted in lesser sentences. When I told you before that I could not sentence you, that was not a challenge for you to bring me further evidence of such crimes. I know you wish to make amends for your actions, but I suggest you find a different avenue for that. If you continue seeking vengeance against yourself the guilt will consume you. I would hate to see you venture any further down that road than you already have."

Conall said nothing but instead lowered his eyes and nodded briefly. "I still feel that I must do more to right my wrongs."

King Elred stepped around his desk and placed his hand on Conall's shoulders. "You have done enough. I will not further condemn you for doing what was needed to save the world."

"Forgive my intrusion, Highness. This won't happen again."

"There is nothing for me to forgive, Conall. I would suggest you find a way to rest. You carried this weight for a long time. You deserve to let it go."

Still held by the king, Conall nodded. Emotions surged inside him like flood water behind a dam after a heavy storm, but he held them back. His mind took him to a small cabin in the woods near the College that he built long ago. This cabin served as an escape for him when he needed time away. He would seek solace there, tucked away in the woods and out of sight of others and his own memories. Seeing no further response from the Mage, the king released him and stepped back behind his desk. He rolled his shoulders and adjusted his tunic before sitting down. When Conall didn't move the king's face hardened briefly, and he dismissed Conall who opened a portal and left without saying anything.

On the other side of the portal, Conall stood alone in his single room cabin in the woods. Simple, dark curtains were drawn over both windows. While the darkness that greeted him felt comforting, he opened one set of curtains to allow some light to filter in. There was no sense living like a root vegetable waiting for the harvest. He stepped away from the window and built a fire on the hearth. That done, he sat in the plain, lacquered rocking chair that sat before the fireplace and stared deep into the flames watching as they slowly consumed the wood. He removed the knife, which he grabbed without the king noticing, and studied the pitted blade. He tested the edge with his thumb and frowned at how much it dulled after decades of neglect.

He stood and grabbed a small leather pouch from the mantle and returned to his chair. He removed a whetstone from the pouch and began sharpening the knife. Thoughts swirled in his mind, a tempest of rage, guilt, and shame filling every bit of space within him. The whetstone whispered against the edge of the blade for nearly an hour while he allowed his condemning thoughts to consume him, festering, multiplying. Satisfied with his honing, Conall tested the edge once more with his thumb. A droplet of vibrant red blood seeped from the small nick this gave him. He watched as the blood continued to gather until the tension broke and the blood rushed down his finger and onto his lap. Thoughts continued to flay him from the inside. Whispers from the darkness told him that if others refused to hold him to the consequences spelled out in the law, he would have to do so himself. His gaze went from his thumb, which continued to drip occasionally, to the knife in his hand. The freshly sharpened edge gleamed in the light that sifted through the window, a stark contrast to the rust coating the rest of the knife. He would hold himself accountable for his actions. His hand tightened on the crumbling hilt of the knife.

As he considered the best approach for his punishment, the king's words whispered in his mind. *Others have committed worse atrocities in peace.* That hardly justified his actions. The king likely didn't wish to bring attention to a scandal. *The guilt will consume you.* Emotions surged inside him, the dam that held them back weakened by the barrage he entertained while sharpening his knife. His vision blurred as tears filled his eyes. *You have done enough.* He closed his eyes, and the tears flowed down his face before they too ended up in his lap. His grip loosened but held onto the knife. He opened his eyes and looked at the fire on the hearth. He watched a log collapse, both pieces dropping into the embers beneath and casting a shower of sparks into the chimney.

"I have done enough," he whispered to himself. "I set myself free from this."

He looked at the knife in his hand and at the prick in his thumb which no longer dripped. A dark, nearly black spot replaced the seeping blood as it dried on his finger. He moved the knife over the arm of his chair and fully loosened his grip. The metal clattered against the floor and when the echo settled, he shook his head, hoping to clear away the whirlwind of remorse. He stood from his chair, added wood to the fire to keep it burning for a while longer, and walked toward the window near his bed. He closed the curtains and sat on the edge of his bed. A wall of exhaustion slammed into his body and after slipping off his shoes, he climbed the rest of the way into bed, settled under the blankets, and let himself drift off. Before sleep embraced him, Conall promised himself that when he awoke, he would rest and find a way to break free from this guilt he bore.

...The End...